Lisa Mezta-Lopez is an avid reader of murder/mystery fiction, so it's no surprise that she would find herself taking a year and a half to write her own murder/mystery story with a very good idea of what keeps her attention and interest in that style of storytelling.

Mezta-Lopez was born and raised with five other siblings fifty-nine years ago, in a small city located along the California and Mexico border. Her father moved the entire family to San Diego, California when she was only nine years old. She remained in San Diego most of her life, until she and her daughter moved to live in Las Vegas, Nevada for ten years.

Now back in San Diego again, she currently works from home helping clients over the phone with their auto and home insurance policies. She's worked as a technician repairing copiers, fax machines, and even typewriters. Having the luxury of not commuting anywhere now gives her more time to write and create with her daughter Lauren Elizabeth and spend time with her two cats.

She is thrilled to put her fascination with the whodunit into a story that has never had this type of twist before.

NIGHTSIGHTED

Lisa Marie Mezta-Lopez

NIGHTSIGHTED

V
Vanguard Press

VANGUARD PAPERBACK

© Copyright 2021
Lisa Marie Mezta-Lopez

The right of Lisa M. Mezta-Lopez to be identified as author of this work has been asserted by her in accordance with the Copyright, Designs and Patents Act 1988.

All Rights Reserved

No reproduction, copy or transmission of this publication may be made without written permission.
No paragraph of this publication may be reproduced, copied or transmitted save with the written permission of the publisher, or in accordance with the provisions of the Copyright Act 1956 (as amended).

Any person who commits any unauthorised act in relation to this publication may be liable to criminal prosecution and civil claims for damages.

A CIP catalogue record for this title is available from the British Library.

ISBN 978 1 784659 76 9

*Vanguard Press is an imprint of
Pegasus Elliot MacKenzie Publishers Ltd.*
www.pegasuspublishers.com

First Published in 2021

**Vanguard Press
Sheraton House Castle Park
Cambridge England**

Printed & Bound in Great Britain

Dedication

This book is for the woman who instilled in me the passion that she had for reading, allowing me to use that passion and turn it into writing, my mother Maria. Thank you so much, Mom. I love and miss you every day. With every beat of my heart.

To my wife Jacqueline, thank you for having the patience to allow me the time it took to write this. I love you with all my heart.

To my daughter Lauren, thank you for your inspiration. For your cheering me on, keeping me motivated every day I set forth on this little journey. I adore and love you so much. I'm always going to cheer for you too. No matter where I am. I'm so very proud of you.

To all the readers, the dreamers, and would-be writers, choose life, and never give up. Age truly is just a number.

Chapter 1

What is it about the night sky that makes one just completely disconnect from where they are at that moment, to just gaze at the overwhelming number of stars, and light from them? Amazing how while we go on in our day to day lives, that stars are constantly forming. No matter what we're doing on Earth.

Justin wished at that moment he didn't know what had brought him to be. To be where he is, to be what he is. The sky is all he has to remove himself from all that has brought him here, the endless gaze between prison bars. Bars on a window that represent the limitations of a life he so desperately wanted to get away from. That night sky. Nineteen years on this planet, and this is all he had to show for it. A prison uniform, and regret that should have sunk in way before he murdered a good friend.

There are so many clichés that would explain why he killed: clichés that were just excuses with a fancy name. If only that man had just given him his wallet, he wouldn't have been forced to kill him, and then caught shortly after. No matter how you slice it, he chose to do the deed, and now he must do the time. Twenty-five years would probably go by as though it were fifteen years while he was in prison. To be tried and convicted as an adult didn't help either. Justin knows that if he plays his cards right, he could be out on parole after just seven years. Not so bad, just do your time, and don't make any more enemies.

He never even imagined that he would be caught.

There is the saying that "what you don't know won't hurt you." However, in his case, it was quite the opposite.

Not even remotely close to any stereotypical killer. So yes, what you don't know could indeed hurt you. In his victim's case, die.

Justin didn't have the same worn-out story of coming from a broken home, daddy issues, a loner, nothing that any profiler or shrink would label as a reason for why he did what he did. In fact, he was so off any radar that they don't even know that his latest victim wasn't his only one. He'd killed before. Though he might have been caught this time, he knows they won't catch him next time. Yes, deep down he knows there will be a next time. Although he was only sixteen, he knows he will feed the hunger that has been inside of him since a very early age. What could possibly have planted that seed at the age of only sixteen? A seed that would grow into the quiet serial killer that he is, and he feels, always will be.

Chapter 2

Reflecting on how he ended up in prison, he still can't figure it out. He was your somewhat typical teenager. Sixteen and a know-it-all. Oldest and youngest. Being an only child gives you both titles. Had good friends, good family, nice home to grow up in. Did his chores. Good grades. Parents that work hard for all they have. So, what is missing? Nothing that is at all clear or visible to the naked eye, that's for sure.

Justin didn't even have any complaints. In fact, he loved his life. He especially loved it when he and his dad would spend time hanging out in the garage tinkering with his dad's hobby of rebuilding motorcycles.

"So, what new and grand things did you learn in school today?" asked his dad.

"Oh, nothing new or grand. Just the typical stuff. You know, what do you call it? The three R's? Reading, Writing, and Arithmetic? Why is that anyway? Only one of those words starts with an R." Justin replied.

"Who knows, sounds good when you say it all together anyway, doesn't it?" his dad said while snickering a bit.

"Yeah, I guess so. All the same, nothing special

today. I'm just waiting until I can get into some more fun stuff, like mechanical-related stuff. Things I may actually use later on in life. I don't see you or Mom really applying everything you learned. How often do you use geometry in your everyday life? I'll bet it's not often."

"Well, we may not use it the way it was taught, but it's in there. You'd be surprised how everything is connected. You've heard of 'six degrees of Kevin Bacon'? Well think of it like that. Though you may not see how it relates, or how it is relevant, it's there if you connect all the dots."

"I guess so. I still don't get it. You can remind me again in about fifteen years, about it all being relevant. okay?"

"Sure, son, but I can tell you right now, just keep it relevant and you'll do fine. You're doing great now, you don't have any issue with grades or anything, so you must see something that is keeping you interested in it, right?"

"You mean aside from some of the students? Sure."

"Well, those students aren't going to propel you into anything that is going to define who you are, are they? So, I would suggest finding some other way of finding it interesting." What his father didn't realize, nor did Justin at that moment, was that some of those students would be playing a role in defining who he would end up being in his adult life. They just wouldn't be alive after that realization.

Chapter 3

That relevance would soon play a very big role in Justin's existence. People come and go so much in one's life that one never knows if they will leave any kind of impression. Time can either work with you, by giving you the opportunity of knowing more about those you associate yourself with, or against you by not leaving any possibility of a chance to know them at all. Time in Justin's day-to-day held no pattern. There was no time management. He either got to know fellow students well enough to call them friends, or time would simply be non-existent and stand still when those very students never had the chance to see their next birthday.

He and Paul got along great. They'd known each other for a couple of years. A few classes together, hanging out at home playing video games. Typical teenage boy routines. They even spent time with Justin's dad in the garage tooling around with the motorcycle.

What drives someone to commit such a heinous crime such as murder? Genes, lifestyles, society, the Environment? Who knows? Something so simple as enjoying someone else's company during the day, and then deciding that the person you consider to be a friend should no longer exist come night time.

Justin could find no rhyme or reason. He and Paul had spent that Saturday at home, enjoying a barbecue with the family, riding bikes around the neighborhood, and just being typical young men. There was an abandoned house a few blocks away that was the perfect spot to do whatever one wanted to do, without the intervention of any adults. Maybe that abandoned home was cursed. That would explain why Justin somehow convinced Paul to show off just how tough he was. Rope and rafters, never a good combination if evil decides to reside in someone's soul.

"I bet I could swing myself out of a noose," Justin said. "If I toss that rope around one of the rafters in the garage, and you kick out a box that I'll stand on once I get the noose around my neck, then I can swing myself out it; would you do it too for $50?"

"You're crazy! You're taller and skinnier than me. It'll be easier for you to get free from it. Besides, $50 isn't enough anyway."

"I may be taller and skinnier, but since you're shorter, you have a lower center of gravity. It'll be easy for you to swing out of it. Tell you what, you go first. If you don't swing yourself out as quickly as I think you will, I'll throw in my Xbox One and two games, and I'll help you down. Deal?"

"I don't know. Pretty stupid for us to even be talking about this."

"C'mon. We're sixteen. We're expected to do

stupid stuff," Justin commented with a smirk.

"All right. How are we going to anchor it? You going to hold onto one end of it? If so, you had better get me down fast if I start to turn as blue as Papa Smurf before I can free myself. Tell me again why we're doing this?"

"Yeah, we'll anchor it to that cabinet handle right there. I'll untie it once you get your legs over to that rafter over there. I promise I will get you down if I see you struggling."

"Okay. You damn well better. I will kick your ass once I'm down if you take too long. Let's use that blue plastic milk case to stand on."

Justin grabbed the case, and set it under the rafter that they would be using. Well, the rafter that he knows Paul will be using. He doesn't plan on using it himself at all. While he was setting the case down, Paul grabbed some rope that was in the corner of the garage that they were in. Seemed like it was pretty old rope. Maybe it would just break on its own before Justin would help him down anyway. Maybe.

They both worked on a making a pretty simple noose at one end of the rope. Neither one of them had ever done one before, but they somehow managed to make one after a couple of attempts. It sure didn't look like a typical noose. Not like ones you see on TV anyway. Those would certainly be a lot easier to get out of no doubt. Hollywood magic and all.

"So, once it is around your neck, reach up above

your head with both hands and hold on to the top of the noose part. That way you can lift yourself up and get yourself swinging your legs over to that rafter in front of the one we're going to use. Once you have your legs on it, I'll untie the other end and help you down. It'll be a rush. Just talking about it is a rush, right?"

"I guess so. All right let's do this so we can get home in time for me to set up the Xbox One that you're going to be giving me."

Chapter 4

Paul slowly placed it over his head and around his neck. Anybody with half a brain must know that this was a very stupid thing to play around with it. How much trust did he have where Justin would concerned? He would soon find out; however, he would not survive to regret it.

With the noose somewhat loosely placed around Paul's neck, Justin went over to the other end of the rope and tied it off to one of the garage cabinet handles. He was nervous that the handle would not hold Paul's weight, and that Paul would just end up falling down before what he is hoping would happen takes place.

Either way, he placed a light hold on the rope between Paul and the tied-off end, so that he had the control, and not Paul.

Everything that was taking place was setting his future life in motion. He knew that Paul won't survive, and if by some unforeseen force he did, he'd make sure that Paul didn't have the opportunity to take his anger out on him for it.

This was the moment that defined his life later on in prison. This was the moment that it all happened. The moment that started what would later have him branded a serial killer. Like an animal branded with a hot iron, marked for life.

He watched Paul, eyeballing the distance from where he was standing on that crate, to the rafter he was to swing his legs over to. The dare itself was nothing: it was the rush that started the adrenaline pumping in one's veins. They were both about to burst from it all.

"Okay, get ready to help me down if I can't make the swing," Paul said with a very shaky voice.

"I'm right here, got my hands on the rope just in case."

He knew very well that he wouldn't do anything to help, but he had to say something.

Paul placed his hands as high as he could above the noose, and then kicked the crate out from underneath his feet. Justin held on to the rope just as the cabinet door swung all the way open and just about busted off of its hinges.

Paul started to swing over to the rafter, while holding on as best he could above that small space of rope above his head.

Justin could see that he actually might make it, so he let go.

As soon as he did, Paul's hands slipped off and the noose was now tight around his neck. He dangled at first, then his face turned blood red.

Justin looked deeply into Paul's eyes, deep enough to almost see the blood cells congregate and run around trying to break free. The pleading, the begging, the fear, all there. None of which needed to be spoken with words.

After a few minutes of struggling, he hung there, motionless. Just a slight sway. Slight enough to mimic a wind chime hanging on a porch. Except there was no sound. Just the sound of leaves being swirled around on the floor.

There was Paul. Like a Halloween decoration. Still. Lifeless. He was a good friend. About the only person that Justin didn't mind being around. Deep down Justin knew that it would come to this. That gnawing in his gut. That indescribable urge. That "what is like to kill someone" feeling. And here it was, in front of him.

He stared at him for a while, but once the thrill subsided and nothing further would happen then and there, he walked away. Leaving Paul to have the garage to himself. Not taking him down, not changing the layout of anything there. Just walking away. Even though he left Paul there, Paul would not leave him. He would learn that as the years went by.

Paul would be the first of five names that would leave a mark on him. A mark that no one would have, or could have, put on him.

It was Paul's name that would appear on his skin in dark black ink on his back. Yes, a mark. A tattoo, really. It was a reminder of who he had removed from this earth. He didn't ask for it. He didn't ask for it. Yet there it was. It would be the first to appear on his skin, simply because Paul was his first. The others would be there too.

What unseen force or black magic or curse could have done that to him? Why him? Why not others in the prison? There must be a reason. An explanation. Everything happens for a reason, but what possible logical reason could there be for this to happen to him? The answer would be one that he had never expected. One that would affect him more than anything else in his life. That answer would lead him on a journey that he would never expect to take.

That journey would begin with the death of his mother.

Chapter 5

It took some time before he would be caught, tried and convicted for Paul's murder. Like bread crumbs, all the little things, pieces, trails, snippets of that day led to Justin. Never once denying the things that took place on that day. No explanation given. Accepting the fate that followed and the unexpected turn of events that would then lead Justin to realize how something so dark and horrible would actually shape why it all took place to begin with.

Having only spent fifteen years of a twenty-five-year sentence behind bars, Justin had but one thing on his mind when he was released. Find out the details of his mother's death. After that, then he would focus on how Paul's name became a mark on his body, and why.

His father, David, picked him up, and took him to the same home that he left all those years ago. The only piece missing was his mom.

"I guess now that you're over twenty-one I can offer you a beer," said his dad once they walked in the front door.

"Sure. It'll be a first for me too," Justin replied, realizing how even something so small as having a beer was such a huge thing to him.

"Yeah, that's true. Your mom would probably say you were still too young to have one. With you here now, this place won't seem so dark for me now. I wish you didn't have to find out about her death the way you did. Especially not being here with your family. I don't have too much to tell you, because the police are still stumped on who did it."

"You mean they haven't done anything about her murder?"

"No, I mean they gave up. There was little to no evidence left behind for them to use. Whoever killed her made sure of that."

"There has to be something for them to go by. I can't imagine whoever killed her would be smart enough to not leave anything behind. Nobody from this town anyway. I'm sorry I wasn't here, Dad. I would have given anything to be here for you, and for Mom. Maybe she'd still be here."

"Don't blame yourself. I had enough blame for us all after she was killed. I went through every 'what if' scenario I could think of. They got her right after work. She didn't do anything different. Even broad daylight couldn't keep the assholes from doing what they did."

"Well, I'm going to talk to the police about what they do know. I'm going to be a thorn in their side. If being incarcerated taught me anything, it taught me patience, and also, that there is no intelligent criminal out there. They left a trail somehow, and I intend to find it and follow it straight to them."

Chapter 6

Daylight took on a whole new feeling for Justin. Even though it wasn't the first time he had greeted the day from the same home he'd left as a child, it was as if he were seeing for the first time. Fresh eyes, fresh take on all of his surroundings. His room was left exactly as it was as he left it. His teenage years were frozen in time on the walls. To have missed out on all of the teenage angst that comes with puberty, all the high school drama, all the typical high school shenanigans, only to have to go through it without friends, with guys that knew nothing other than what it was like to be in prison.

He didn't share with his dad the marking on his body that spelled out Paul's name. Nor did he share with him that he wasn't the only one with markings like that. It was something that not only happened to him, but to every other inmate in the prison he left. The only thing was that he was the only one to see those markings. All of the victim's names on the bodies of those who played judge, jury and executioner. Only thing was, those whose roles were considered to be the executioners, didn't even know they had them. Justin would be the only person to see them. And seemingly, only in the dark. Like shining beacons in the night. Branded. Why was he chosen to be the one and only pair of eyes to see so many names? So many lives cut short. Why him? What good reason could there possibly be? Not sure how his dad would react, so he kept that secret to himself for a while. Not like his dad would likely believe him anyway. He did know that there has to be an explanation for it appearing on his body, and on the bodies of all those still incarcerated. And why appear just before his release, after being in prison all those years? What he didn't know yet, anyway, was the role Paul's name appearing and the death of his mother, would play in his release from prison. These two distinctly different facets of his life would eventually become the one thing that would define who he was.

Walking into the kitchen was like taking baby steps again. Although it was very much the same as when he last saw it, it definitely had a whole new feeling to it. He still saw so much of the little touches that only his mother could leave. Down to the little red rooster dishtowels. Even the red rooster cookie jar was still on top of the fridge. However, it was no longer out of his reach. So many things the same, and yet so many changes as well.

He missed all of the little nuances that make a home a home. He still sees his mom's old owl apron that she always wore in the kitchen, whether she needed it or not. It was a staple for her. Her thing was owls, but she also loved pairing owls with her red rooster knickknacks. It was all those little things that he loved seeing again.

How he missed his mom. Feeding the unexplainable evil hunger that began all those years ago might have robbed him of seeing her now, but now, it fueled the fire that burned deep down in order to find who killed her. He had already convinced himself that he wouldn't leave it up to the police detectives to track down her killer, or killers: he was going to do whatever it takes to find them himself if he had to.

He would soon have help that wouldn't even be in human form. Help that was right now beginning to take shape. Help that began all those years ago when he was arrested. The kind of help that nobody could ever have seen before. Yet it was something that would allow him to help not only himself and his dad cope with her loss, but others as well. Others that, like him, were looking for answers, for a resolution. Most of all, justice in the form of revenge.

Chapter 7

His father joined him in the kitchen after a couple of hours. Justin was eager to begin filling in the blank spaces of his life away from home.

"You got up early," said his dad after joining Justin at the table with his coffee.

"Not that early. I slept in, compared to the hour that we were up in prison. I'm just relishing the softness of the mattress. I probably would have stayed in bed longer, but didn't want the day to get away from me," Justin replied while walking over to get more coffee.

"Yeah, I can totally understand the mattress part. That had to be rough. Not to mention the noise around there, huh?"

"The noise you definitely get used to. The so-called mattress, not so much."

"I bet. So, what do you have planned for today? Want to take a ride around town, visit friends you haven't seen?"

"Given what I did, it certainly didn't leave me with many friends. I kept in touch with some while locked up, but since my life wasn't going anywhere, or changing at the time, they moved on. So, I've been out of touch with just about everyone."

"Sorry to hear that. You know, your mom never gave up on you. People around here may have given her the side glances and whispers from time to time, but she never let any of that bother her. You're her son, and no matter what, she loved and believed in you always. Me too."

"I know. Thanks, Dad. I will never, ever be able to show just how much I wish I could take back all the events that landed me in prison. I'm so sorry to have let you both down."

"I know you are. At first, I was angry. Very disillusioned by what you had done. As a parent, you know, you blame yourself first. Your mom did too. The typical cliché of what did we do wrong? Where did we fail you? Was it something we could have prevented? After a while, we stopped trying to figure out what happened. We turned our anger that built up from all the people hating on us, on you, into just being there to show our support for you. We know that we were good parents. We did the best we could. Whatever it is, was, that drove you to kill the five individuals that you did, we know deep down it wasn't because of what we did or didn't do. We realized that we couldn't find anyone or anything to blame it on. You had choices. We instilled in you to always make the right choice. Whatever possessed you to make the wrong choices was something beyond your mom and I. There are no answers I know. But, just know that your mom never gave up on you. I do know she must be incredibly happy to see us talking here at the table together, after all these years."

"Thanks, Dad. I will do everything I can to make it up to you. To her too. Though she isn't here, I know she is watching over us. I can't tell you how much I appreciate all your support," Justin said while going to get another cup. "Would you like me to make you another cup?"

"No, you go ahead. I've got some errands in town. Hobby stuff, you know. I still tinker with bikes to this day. You're welcome to come along."

"Actually, I'm going to hang around here for a while. Check out the classifieds for a job."

"You know you can do that all online now," his dad said with a chuckle.

"Oh yeah, forgot about the whole technology kick. I guess technology has changed a lot in the past fifteen years."

"Yeah, took me a while to get used to it myself. I am probably right there with you as far as my learning curve with it all," his dad said while pushing away from the kitchen table.

"Guess I have some catching up to do," said Justin.

"Well, you're not alone there. If you want, and only if you want to, I still have the cell phone your mom used. I never turned it back in. All I have to is give the cell phone company a call and have them reactivate it, or whatever they call it. That way, if you need something from town you can always let me know. I will warn you though, I haven't done much texting. I'm more of a 'let me hear your voice' kind of guy."

"That would be nice, thanks. And no worries with the texting part. It's a learning curve for me too," Justin replied with a laugh.

"Great. Why don't I just take it with me then, and I'll stop by the cell phone place and just have them do what they have to do there? I'll just give it to you when I get back."

"Sounds good. Thanks."

With that, Justin's dad grabbed his keys off the old owl key holder that was still on the wall next to the entry of the kitchen, and headed out the front door.

Chapter 8

Justin took this time he had alone to reacquaint himself with this house he called home all those years ago.

He went upstairs and strolled into his parent's room. He could still see himself running into that same room and jumping into bed with them. How he missed those days. The room looked pretty much the same. Nice to see that his dad kept everything very similar to how it looked the last time he saw it. Furniture was a bit newer, but the layout was just as he remembered it to be. His mother's passion for reading was evident in a book still on her nightstand that his dad had never removed. A book by one of her favorite writers, Danielle Steele. Family photos still displayed on the dresser. One of his favorites was still up, one of him and his mom on his very first day of school. He barely remembered having the photo taken of course, but could remember all the fun days following that. Making new friends, new and exciting things to learn. Memories cut short a lifetime ago.

His parents were never very religious, but he could still remember an occasional Sunday at church with them. Not every Sunday, but on occasion. They did go more often when he was much younger. Trying to instill a strong belief. A belief in a faith that they grew up with themselves. They were so busy trying to keep him along that faithful path that they lost a little of it themselves. The church on Sunday mornings as a family weren't as frequent. Maybe they went more after he went to prison. Trying to get answers for all they felt they did wrong. Maybe. He smiled when he saw some of the only photos of when they did go as a family to church. Easter Sunday. Festivities tailored around such a holy day, but yet also tailored around painting eggs, hiding eggs, finding eggs, eggs which he never realized as a child that were to have been left by a giant rabbit. Funny how that worked. Thinking of that made him realize he would never be passing that tradition on to his own children. He might be reformed now that he wasn't in prison any more, but not reformed enough to have a family. He was just as happy reliving the memories he has with his own family. He didn't have time for a family now anyway. Too much to do.

He walked around the bedroom a bit more. Walking through their closet. Most of his mother's clothes gone, of course. A few pieces of clothing remained hanging. Couldn't blame his father for wanting to hold on to all he could, to go along with his memories, of the only woman he would ever spend his life with. Her vanity still displayed her favorite pieces of jewelry, favorite perfumes. Hairbrush, makeup, hand-held mirror. As if she had just walked out of the room after using all of what remained.

He felt compelled to touch each piece of whatever was there. How his dad must ache seeing that day in and day out. Or maybe, unlike other survivors like his dad, this was the only way he knew how to get through each day. Who was to say how one should get through life after the loss of a loved one? Especially a loss that was not expected. He smiled at seeing a special little box that she kept for all of her lipsticks. A shade for every occasion. One of her biggest traits. Never at a loss for lipstick. In every shade of her favorite color too, red. The darker the red, the better. He never felt she needed so many. She always seemed to want to buy a new tube of it whenever they went to the store together. Whether she needed it or not. She wanted to make sure she never ran out, he guessed.

Looking around he noticed a calendar hanging. It was a calendar from just two years ago. Thinking back two years ago, he tried to picture he and his father's lives at that time. Trying to understand why it was still there. And why July? The only significance July held to him was July of last year. That was when he noticed Paul's name appearing on him. How could his dad possibly know about that? Could his dad know without his telling him about that? If so, what role could his dad possibly play in Paul's name showing up anyway? He stared long and hard at the calendar as if the answer were written on it somewhere. Time stopped for his father apparently in July two years ago. Then it hit him, of course: his mom, his hero. Taken from him, and his dad in July, two years ago. Two long, but very short, years ago. How could these two very significant and vastly different parts of his life happen in the same month? More importantly, why? He couldn't remember the exact day he noticed Paul's name, but he had to believe his mom being snatched away from them in the same month was some sort of unexplainable coincidence. One he now knew would be his purpose in the days ahead. One that he felt would hold the answer to the question of why Paul's name was on him. As well as why he was the only person to see it and the other four names. One that would begin tomorrow. Where it all began for him. The police station.

Chapter 9

Walking through the entrance to the police station gave him a really odd feeling. More so because he thought he would never be able to freely walk into it, let alone through the entrance. It was a very freeing moment, though. One that gave him a certain feeling of determination.

He didn't feel a need to tell his dad right away what he would be doing there. He hadn't planned on reaching out to the police anyway. He just decided that they'd be the only obvious starting point. If they didn't give him the answers, or help he needed, he'd set out on his own.

He walked up to the front counter and asked to speak to whoever he needed to in order to find out who was, or had been, placed on his mother's murder investigation.

"What's your name, hun?" asked the clerk.

"My name is Justin Anthony Ancin. My mother was Marnie Isabel Ancin. She was murdered two years ago July 23rd. I was incarcerated at the time of her murder, and would like to speak with whomever was the lead investigator at that time."

"I wish I could say I could immediately help you, but there'll be a few steps we have to take before I can."

Justin could most definitely detect that expected hint of judgement in her voice, simply because he mentioned he was in prison at one time. He knew he would be met with some apprehension, so he was ready for it. He just hoped that he would be patient enough to let whoever it was, take the reins and get him to the answers he needs.

All eyes on him, or so it seemed. He had jumped through the short necessary hoops, and the small portion of red tape in order to get to the right person. No matter what, he would find the person or persons responsible for taking his mom away from him and his father.

"Justin? Justin Ancin?" spoke a man in a dark blue dress shirt, tie, and dress slacks, wearing a badge attached to his belt.

"Yes, I'm Justin," he said while standing and extending his hand to the gentleman calling for him.

The gentleman shook Justin's hand and said, "My name is Detective Hewitt. Why don't we step over to my desk where we can talk a bit about why you are here? I see you already have one of our fancy visitors' badge, huh?"

Justin smiled while looking at the laminated badge clipped to his shirt pocket. "Yeah. Thanks for taking the time to talk to me."

"Of course. Our clerk said you were looking to speak to someone about your mom's case, is that right? Here, have a seat." He offered Justin the chair across from him while he took his seat behind his desk.

Justin sat down, and took in all the sights and sounds around him. Detective Hewitt's office was located pretty close to everything that one would expect to see and hear in a police station. Phones constantly ringing, conversations that seemed to go nowhere. The smell of coffee permeated the air: not only fresh, but burnt too. His desk had the obligatory family pictures. A couple of windows offered just enough of a distraction on the outside for when the mundane and frustrations became too much. Awards and certificates graced the two walls that surrounded the room. Several other photos with community leaders, and notable law enforcement dignitaries. He went ahead and took a seat and gathered his thoughts. Though he knew what he wanted to get done, it was these first steps that were always a little daunting.

"Yeah. I was unfortunately not in a good place, both figuratively and physically, when she was murdered. I actually heard while I was behind bars."

"I will say, I took the liberty of reading up on you a bit before I came out to get you. Safe to say that being locked up made an impression on you? And not in the way most people think, right?" The detective let that question just hang there, allowing Justin to continue thinking about how he wanted to start this.

"Yeah, it was definitely humbling and scary all at once. It certainly wasn't something that I had planned on doing before the age of twenty-one, I'll say that much." Justin replied. Still feeling a bit awkward at how to start the conversation and where to go with it.

"Well, good to see that you came through unscathed. At least that is how it looks from here. I will also say that it's not every day that I sit behind my desk here, engaged in a conversation with an ex-con. You probably felt like there was a flood of spotlights on you when you got here."

"That's an understatement. Nothing like feeling that every pair of eyes in the room is focused and set on you."

"So, let's get to the meat and potatoes of why you're here shall we?" Detective Hewitt grabbed a notebook and a pen, ready to take down any info that Justin had to relay.

Justin, for whatever reason, was very nervous. Should he tell him the main reason why he felt he would be able to lend more to his mother's case? The names, on not only his body, but on all the other inmates as well? How he knew that if he were led in the right direction, he would find the cowards that took away his mother? He did know that he wouldn't be able to do it alone. Time for the craziness to commence.

Chapter 10

"So here is the thing, Detective. I am about to tell you some pretty crazy shit. Just hear me out, and maybe, just maybe we can get to the asshole, or assholes, that killed my mom. Two years ago, mid-July, I woke up one day and noticed some rather strange changes to my body. As I looked in my mirror, it was as if someone had branded me like cattle in the middle of the night."

"What do you mean branded? Like someone took a cigarette to you? How could you not feel a burning cigarette butt?" The detective was already feeling like his time was being wasted.

"No, not like a cigarette burn. More like a tattoo. But not just a tattoo, it was a name. Paul Adams. Along with the date that Paul died." Justin waited for the detective to kick him out of his office.

"Paul Adams? Wait, you mean to tell me that the kid you killed is now a tattoo on you?" Probably the most farfetched thing he has probably ever heard in his twenty-seven-year career.

"Yes, that is exactly what I am saying. And before you say anything like why would someone do that to me, let alone not feel it being done to me, let me also say that I am the only person that can see it." Justin wished that the coffee down the hall wasn't just coffee at this point.

Detective Hewitt slid his chair away from his desk, and stood up. With one hand on his hip and the other rubbing the back of his neck, he looked out the window for a moment or two before redirecting his glare right into the middle of Justin's eyes. He truly thought he had heard it all, until now.

"Listen, Justin. You know, guys go into prison all cocky and so full of themselves, then while they're in there they 'find God,' you know? I've had guys get released just to do the same thing that put them there in the first place. Guys that have now become contributing, involved, and very community driven members of society. I have to say that this is the first time I've heard of a guy coming out of prison with a tattoo of their victim, and not knowing how it got there." He found himself pacing the room now not sure whether to believe Justin, ask him to leave, or whether to just listen to what he had to say with an open mind. He chose the latter.

"Detective, I came here because I wanted to find out what happened with my mother's case. My dad doesn't have the emotional stamina to do the same. When I found out about her death, I wanted to break through the walls no matter the consequence, and go out and kill the person that took her. Took a few months for it to sink in, not to mention quiet the rage inside of me because of it."

The detective walked over to his little mini fridge and grabbed a Coke, wishing he had some rum to go with it. "Would you like a Coke? Something tells me you have some talking to do and your throat will certainly get dry."

Justin took the Coke and continued with his story.

"Okay, just hear me out. In fact, look at my back." He took off his shirt and turned his back towards the detective.

"I don't see anything," said the Detective while frowning as he stared at Justin's bare skin.

"Exactly. About a week or so before I was released, it happened. As soon as I saw Paul's name, I immediately bitched out my cell mate, asking him what the hell was going on. After a few heated words, it was clear he didn't see what I saw. I thought since I was going to be released soon that I wouldn't rock the boat with him and just play it cool and chalk it up to my anxiety at getting out. Paul's name was not there the day before, and my cell mate thought I had lost it. That night I was having a hard time sleeping because of what happened, so as I just lay in bed, I started to see a glow in the cell and couldn't tell where it was coming from. As I looked around, I noticed it coming from above me. My cell mate's bunk. He had a name on his back too, and it was glowing. I woke him up and asked if he could see anything lighting up the cell, and he said 'no' and told me to basically go to hell and go back to sleep. As the next week rolled by, getting closer to my release, I started to see names glowing from other inmates as I looked out to the other cells around me. I honestly thought I had completely lost my mind. The thing is, it's only at night of course, because they glow. I mean, I haven't seen anything during the day. Nobody sees any names except me. And nobody else sees the glowing either. I know it sounds like the most unbelievable thing you've ever heard, but it's true. I really need you to believe me."

"So, now you're telling me that you not only see your victim's name on your body, but now you're seeing them on everyone else's too? And the names… light up … or glow?" Detective Hewitt was two minutes from kicking him out of his office, but thought he'd give him a little bit longer to build on this huge story he was being given.

"That's exactly what I am telling you. Look, I know you have no reason to believe me…"

"You're right I don't. By my having spent the amount of time it took to listen to that I know I could have spent it in a way more productive manner."

"So, hear me out, please. I may not have any credibility in your eyes, or world, I know that, but you're the first person I have told this to. I don't have any friends outside of prison, if you want to call them that. I can't tell my dad because I know for certain he won't believe me."

"And what makes you feel confident enough to think that I would?"

"Because I am pretty sure you would have kicked my ass out of your office by now."

Detective Hewitt sat back and stared Justin down before getting up to pace in front of his window for a few minutes, resigning himself to the fact that Justin was right. He would have kicked him out by now. Something had him believing his ridiculous story. After thinking about Justin's story, he realized he had a story for Justin too, and after listening to Justin's he was just as confident that Justin had to believe his too.

Chapter 11

Detective Hewitt told Justin to stay in his office for a few minutes while he stepped out into another office briefly. He was gone for approximately twenty minutes, which was almost too much time to be alone with his thoughts in a police station, of all places. He was just hoping he had made the right decision in making a detective the first person to share his story with.

Detective Hewitt finally comes back in and tells Justin to get up and go with him. He then grabs his coat jacket from the rear of his desk chair and starts to put it back on as Justin starts to slowly stand up.

"Why? Where are we going?" Justin asks. Confusion written all over his face. Feeling both startled, and concerned, as to what was happening.

"You didn't think you could just come in here, and drop some story about seeing victims' names on people, yourself included, without some sort of proof, did you? Let me ask you, do you see the word sucker across my forehead?"

"No, of course not." Justin quietly answers. Feeling somewhat like a child about to get sent into the corner of the room.

"Exactly. Which is why you and I are taking a quick trip down to the county jail. You're going to tell me if you see any names on folks that have already been tried and convicted for their crimes. I won't tell you anything about them, or their cases, and you're going to tell me what you see."

"Okay, yeah, sure. Whatever it takes for you to help me. I'm not lying though. I wish I was, but I'm not."

"I'll be the judge of that. Let's go."

They spend approximately 2 hours at the county lockup, and much to Detective Hewitt's surprise, Justin does indeed point out names on at least 5 different inmates that are incarcerated for not only homicide, but second-degree murder as well. This truly blows the mind of the good detective.

"Okay. You've got me pretty speechless. Which is not easy."

"I told you. Now, will you help me?"

Detective Hewitt doesn't say anything, except for "Alright, let's go back to the station. I've got something else for you."

When they arrive back at the station, Detective Hewitt instructs Justin to go wait for him in his office. He then goes down the hall, away from his office, and heads to a different room for the next ten to fifteen minutes or so.

Just as he was seriously having second thoughts about seeking out the good detective's help, and was about to leave, Detective Hewitt comes back in, carrying a couple boxes of files. The name "Florentelli, Carla R./Ancin, Marnie Isabel" with the date of July 23rd, 2010 written in bold black letters and numbers on the end of each box.

"All right, kid. I've listened to you, now you can listen to me. If you want my help in finding your mom's killer, then maybe you can help me too. How much do you know about your mom's life before you were born?" he asked while taking the lid off of one of the first boxes, and slowly started taking files out, and placing them in between the two of them on his desk.

"Wait a minute, I'll help you with what I know, but before I do, who is Carla R. Florentelli? And why do you have her files with my mom's files?" Detective Hewitt didn't answer him, but just stared at him. With that stare he was met with silence as well. Just enough silence to determine that that was why he was asked how much he knew about his mom before he was born. "Was this Carla woman killed at the same time my mom was? Did they know each other? Do you think this Carla woman is connected to my mom's killers too? What is the connection? Tell me."

"So, by all your questions in the past few seconds, I'm going to take an educated guess and say you didn't know much about your mom before you came along," he said while taking a seat back behind his desk. He held out a couple of files in front of him and handed them over to Justin. "I would offer you something a bit stronger than a Coke, but, seeing as we are in a police station, that might be frowned upon."

"What am I reading, Detective? Not to mention why? And let me first say thank you. By you bringing these boxes in here, guess that means your little test back at the county jail, means you believe me and are willing to help."

"By my bringing in these boxes doesn't exactly mean I completely believe you. That remains to be seen. But yes, the county jail helped. I would like it if you could shed a little light on this then I'm sure we can work something out that would benefit us both.

"What you're looking at are the case files of one murder. One person. Two different names. Carla Rose Florentelli, a.k.a. Marnie Isabel Ancin, your mom. I'll try to condense it for you so that you can take time to absorb it later on at home. Your mom's true birth name wasn't the name you knew growing up. She changed it when she was around twenty, shortly before she met your dad. The reason she changed it was because she was on the run. When she was a teenager she met and married a good-looking, streetwise kid by the name of Marco Romeo Florentelli. He was seventeen when they met, she was fifteen and a half. He smoothed his way into her family. When he was about eighteen, he swore to your grandparents that they would never have to worry about her, that he would treat her like the princess she was, and that he wanted to marry her. Your grandparents saw this as an opportunity for her to get a paid education, a better roof over her head and a better life than what they could provide for her. What they didn't know, nor did your mom, was that he came from a very prominent mob family in Florida. Marco swept her off her young feet, then swept her family off theirs. They gave their consent for the two of them to get married and by her seventeenth birthday she and Marco were married. He did take good care of her by all accounts, good school, nice roof over her head; she didn't have a care in her young world at all. When she got her high school diploma, we believe she was looking to go to college, but Marco wanted her home. She stayed home, started to question why he kept such late hours at a job she was always led to believe was an insurance-related job. Her questions led her to eavesdropping on conversations, we believe, and those conversations must have been about his real job… a prominently held position in his family's mobster-styled career ladder. She had heard too much, more than likely, and decided to figure out a way to leave that wouldn't lead back to her once she was gone. We do know for a fact that she contacted some folks that practiced some form of witchcraft, or occult practices of some sort. They confirmed that she had asked for help with casting spells. Feeling that she wouldn't get any help from the law, due to them likely being on a payroll for his family. We have reason to believe that it was sometime after that when she put her escape plan into play." He let that all just hang out there, to allow a little bit of time for Justin to absorb some of what he was just told. It was as if the entire police station fell silent after he was finished. Not to mention, it got eerily quiet inside his windows too.

Justin couldn't believe what he had just heard. He didn't want to. "What I'm looking at and hearing, Detective, are scenes from a life that I can't begin to place my mother into. You're telling me that my whole life, our whole life, both me and my father's, was a farce? Did my father know this about her?" He got up and started to pace around the room.

"I'm pretty sure he didn't know up until we told him, once we discovered it ourselves during our investigation. I don't know how much time you and your dad have spent with each other since your release, but it's obviously not been long enough for him to be the one to fill you in on this instead of me. Needless to say, I'm sure what we told him is still sinking in. Did you tell him you were coming over here today?"

"No, I didn't. I didn't really think I'd be coming here today. I knew I had to start somewhere, just figured this would be the best place to start. I sure as hell didn't expect this." He placed the files he had been reading and scanning through back into the box they came out of. "I'm not sure if this was a good idea or not, my coming to you guys for help, but I'm going to take a few days to let this sink in and talk to my father before I do anything further. I don't expect you to help me, let alone completely believe me. I guess if I want you to believe me, I'm going to have to believe you too. I just don't have the mindset I need to really take this in right now. So, I'm going to go do something I haven't done yet, and head over to the closest bar and buy myself a drink. I need something strong to chase that soda with, and strong enough to soak up what you just told me. I'll be in touch." He stood up and extended his right hand in order to shake the detective's hand and thanked him for his time.

Detective Hewitt stayed standing and watched him head down the hallway towards the main entrance. He placed the lid back onto box one of two, but instead of taking them back to the store room, he left them on top of his desk. He knew he hadn't seen the last of Justin. He knew it, and so did Justin. Either way, he knew that he would be going through those files again, only this time he would have Justin with him when he did. How much could he believe about what Justin told him, and showed him at the county jail. Invisible names. Names that only he saw? Names that glowed? What kind of insane sci-fi story was that? Could he really believe this ex-con? What kind of person made up such a story? Maybe it was just that, a story. Told to him in order to persuade him to once again pursue a killer that had been invisible themselves for the past two years. Pretty convincing what he saw him do either way, so how could he not believe him. Well, one thing for sure, this case had just taken a turn, and with Justin's help, it may be a hairpin turn.

Chapter 12

Justin spent the next two weeks just getting used to the outside world again. Used to his old home again, and just letting his freedom sink in a little at a time. What he hadn't let sink in yet was the story that Detective Hewitt had given him about his mother. A previous life, a former name, witchcraft? What the hell happened to her? He spoke at length with his dad about everything the detective told him, while his dad remained silent the entire time. David hadn't told Justin about Marnie's supposed previous life. Namely because he was still coming to grips with it himself.

Apparently, his mom had left Florida under the new name of Marnie Isabel Adams. They met through mutual friends at a college she had put herself through with money she had saved. They fell in love, married, and at the age of twenty-five had Justin. Nothing extraordinary about their story. No red flags for David when they met and started their life together.

"Well, that's all good to hear. I mean, if she hadn't left Florida the way she did, I wouldn't be here right now. So, there is that." He said to David. "I wonder if she realized that her new initials turned out to be M.I.A. once you two married. I never noticed that before. Heh."

He says as they both share a light chuckle upon that realization. "Thanks again for the cell phone. I've given myself a crash course on it, and I think I have it figured out for the most part." He said while making breakfast for the both of them.

"Yeah, no problem." David got coffee for himself, and poured a cup for Justin as well. "I know I'm still sorting through all that we've been through, so I can't begin to imagine how it is for you. Leaving prison life, and beginning your adult life with all that you now know." He set a couple plates out, utensils, and the two hot cups of coffee. "When Detective Hewitt first told me about your mom's life before we had met, I didn't want to believe him at all. I thought he made it up as some sort of excuse as to why they didn't have anything on her murder. Some sort of way to distract me away from what they hadn't accomplished. But then it started to make more sense to me as to why I didn't know more about her family." He sat down, while Justin served them both some hash browns, whole wheat toast, scrambled eggs, and some fresh fruit.

Justin pulled his seat in closer to the table while putting some French vanilla creamer in his coffee. "After you learned about mom's past, did you do anything about it? I mean, did you try to find out more about her family, my maternal, and paternal, grandparents, at all?" He took a few moments to once again appreciate what he had before him, still relishing the fact that he no longer had to worry about his food being stolen, or bartering with other inmates for different food.

"At first, I thought about doing some detective work of my own, but, then thought against doing that because I didn't want any second thoughts, regrets, or to even question the twenty plus years we had together. As far as I was concerned, our lives started when we met each other at college." He said in between forkful after forkful of food. "My life as I had known it, pretty much ended that day two years ago, when she was killed. When I knew for a fact that you were going to be released early, that was the best thing that could have happened to me after that. You being released became my main focus. With you here now, that is all I care about." He took in his last forkful of hash browns and left a rather clean plate in front of him. "Thanks for breakfast, son. That was pretty damn good." He rubbed his belly before sliding his empty plate away from him.

"Yeah, of course. Glad you enjoyed it. That was pretty damn good, if I do say so myself. Guess all that cooking in the kitchen for a bunch of hungry inmates paid off." They both smiled and laughed about that. Justin finished the final bites of his food, while David took his plate, and utensils over to the kitchen sink and placed them all inside of it. Pouring himself some more coffee first, he then walked the coffee pot over to Justin's cup and warmed up his serving. "Thanks," said Justin. He set the pot on the table in between them, while sitting back down and enjoying the rest of the morning they had together.

"Listen, I know your mind must be racing with all that you were told by Detective Hewitt, about Mom, and wondering why I didn't say anything to you sooner, but that doesn't change anything about the love and support Mom and I felt and gave to you," said David, hoping that Justin would decide to leave well enough alone.

"I know, and no worries. I'm not going to do anything stupid. I learned my lesson. I am going to talk to Detective Hewitt and mull some things around with him," Justin said as he walked both their now empty coffee cups over to the kitchen sink. "You drink your coffee about as fast as I do mine."

"Heh. Yeah, I tend to do that. Okay, well, I'm going to be here tooling around in the garage as usual. If you need anything let me know." David then stood and patted Justin's right shoulder before walking towards the garage.

"I could use a favor actually. I used most of the cash that they gave me when I was released for cab rides around here, if you can take me to DMV so I can get a driver's license again. I've studied all that I can for it. I'm pretty sure my old one expired." He said trying to make light of an already heavy conversation. "No time like the present to give it a shot."

"Sure son, no problem." He grabs his keys, and they both head over to the red Jeep Wrangler parked in the driveway.

Not doing anything stupid could be translated into

many things. Justin definitely knew the difference now between doing that, and something gratifying. He just hoped that everything he did from now on, would be the latter.

Chapter 13

Justin spent the next few days just enjoying his freedom. He told his dad that he would hit the pavement hard looking for a job once he figured out what it was, he wanted to do for work. Not that he really had the luxury to be choosy, but living with his father did offer him some time to start looking for some answers.

He called Detective Hewitt and asked him to meet him at a local coffee shop. All that studying paid off as he passed his driving test, on paper and behind the wheel. He borrowed his dad's Jeep, and drove over to the little mom and pop shop just a few minutes away. Justin went ahead and grabbed a coffee, pastry, and a quiet little table for them to chat.

Detective Hewitt prepared himself for whatever Justin may throw at him, psyching himself out on the drive over, convincing himself to have an open mind. He was very skeptical at first when Justin had told him his story, but since the detective knew his mom dabbled in things Justin would soon learn about, it didn't take very long for him to let it soak in.

"Thanks for coming to meet me." Justin said to the detective as he slid into the chair across from him.

"Of course, thanks for calling. I admit I didn't think

I would hear from you at all, but I'm glad you took some time for yourself, and time to catch up with your dad. It also helped me as well. Not every day you hear about someone experiencing what you are going through. I thought I would bring some additional info about your mom's case. Thought we could review a few details. Having interviewed your dad in the days after she died, I would love to hear what you have to contribute. Even though you weren't around her at the time, maybe even something as little as a conversation could help." He removed two manila folders from a leather briefcase, before setting the briefcase down on the floor next to his chair. Setting the two folders between them on the table, he stood and told Justin to go ahead and browse through them while he went to get some coffee.

Justin scanned the pages in the first folder, trying to absorb all the information contained in just a few pages. His mother was last seen speaking to a man that appeared to have approached her just a few moments before, while inside the grocery store, she worked at. The man must have known where the security cameras were due to his ability to avoid showing too much of his face to them. They spoke for those few moments inside the store. He appeared to say something to her that caused her to deny whatever it was he said due to her shaking her head "no" to his comment. A few minutes after that, she was observed leaving the store with a couple coworkers, then was approached by another man outside the store near her car. Again, whoever approached her must have had knowledge of the security cameras and hid their identity fairly well. They appeared to speak for a few moments before she walked away with that man out of the view of the cameras. That was the last time she was seen before her body was discovered two days later about three blocks away, strangled and stuffed into a dumpster in an alley where there was only one security camera.

However, it was too far away to get a clear look at either the people who dumped her, or any car they might have driven up in. This seemed to be the makings of looking for that proverbial needle in a haystack, and Justin didn't know which emotion to start feeling first. Anger or the painful unmeasurable loss of a loved one. He chose anger.

As Detective Hewitt set his coffee and pastry down on the table, Justin shut the second folder, which contained the autopsy report and forensic findings from the crime scene, and handed them back to him. He placed both of them back into his leather briefcase before sitting back down.

"I know how difficult reading the details must be for you, but try to be as objective as you can." He lets Justin gather his thoughts for a moment before continuing on. "As you have read, whoever was behind your mom's murder did their homework. They knew where the security cameras were. They knew where she was at that time. They knew what to say to her that would convince her to leave with them. They by all accounts knew her... period."

"And what did the witnesses tell you happened, before the suspects took her away?"

"They only told us that they saw them speaking to each other for a few minutes next to her car, that they appeared to be in a rather involved conversation. They didn't appear to be combative with each other or arguing, so that told us that she must have known them, too. At least from what the eyewitnesses told us. They said that whatever was being said to her seemed to be enough to convince her to leave with the men without a second thought."

"So, that's probably why nobody paid much attention to them since she probably seemed pretty calm in whatever was being said to her." Justin tried to wrap his mind around what he was hearing. What could possibly convince her to remain calm without calling for help? They had to have threatened her badly enough to the point of leaving her no choice but to comply. "They must have threatened to kill her if she didn't do exactly what they said, right?"

"More than likely yes, but what our investigation pieced together was that it was more than just her life they threatened: it was yours and your father's too."

"What the hell you talking about? Why would total strangers want to hurt any of us? Wait a minute. You said that my mother was married before, to some mob guy, right? So, are you saying that her murder has to do with that guy somehow? If so, then why the hell is her case closed by now? You know who he is and why she left in the first place, why not just arrest the guy?" Justin was now already thinking about reverting to that part of his brain that would lead him to do something deemed stupid again.

"Hold on and calm down. We have every reason to believe he was involved, but as you know we have to follow the leads and piece all of our evidence together in order to have a solid case against him. We got as far as we could by finding out about her previous identity, her previous marriage, her previous life entirely. But even with all that we found out about her life prior to who she was when she died, we were unable to bring in Marco Florentelli because he, um… disappeared. Along with any trail leading to him, or the men who may have done his dirty work. We can only speculate that the guys that did Marco's dirty work and murdered your mother are probably hiding out with him. Still protecting him. Somewhere. But with no trail leading to them, obviously." Hewitt let Justin soak in what he just said. "Look, I want to catch the bastards just as much, if not more than you, believe me. We have to be smarter than them in order to do that, though. They may have outsmarted us by going into hiding, but eventually we will catch up."

"Okay. So, exactly how much did you find out, and how did your trail come to a dead end?"

"After she died, we eliminated your father as having anything to do with her death. He told us how they met, and their life after that. What struck us as odd was that he said she was always very reluctant to talk about her family; about her parents, if she had any siblings, where she grew up. He said it was always something that she never felt comfortable talking about. That led us to wanting to dig deeper into her past. So, we started with where they met. College. We spoke to the admissions board, and they told us that she didn't have any family at all. She was living with friends. She worked part-time for living expenses, but paid cash for her tuition. Everything just didn't seem to add up. There wasn't any paper trail, no credit cards, no checking or savings account. She always paid cash for everything."

"Well, she didn't just pop up out of thin air. How did you find out where she came from if she didn't have any paper trail to follow?"

The detective reached into his leather briefcase for another file. "We figured we'd check with buses, trains, flights in at that time, near and around the time she would have arrived. She did go so far as to tell Admissions and her friends that she came in from Florida but didn't really elaborate, so that was what led us to trace her back to Miami. Took some digging and time, but that was what led us there." He shared some of the information from the other file, and photos that were archived from security cameras in and around her life in Miami, and ultimately her trip, and life, to Dulzura, California. Where she and David ended up living, and raising Justin.

"So, what all of this telling me is I need to go to Miami," Justin replied as he perused the photos and pages. Looking at everything on them sent his mind into a tailspin. How could his mom, a woman that gave and displayed nothing but love and support unconditionally have had another life entirely? An entirely different person, two names, two vastly different lives and lifestyles. It was enough to make a person go mad. He decided then and there that he wouldn't waste any more time and make plans to go to Miami and start digging for answers.

Detective Hewitt stared Justin right in his eyes, leaning over the little table, getting right in his face. "No, this isn't something I am showing you simply to make you decide on a trip out there. We did that, followed what little leads we could, and hit a dead end once we found out about Marco and his connections. They're pretty guarded even to this day about his life."

"You know as well as I do that anyone even remotely connected with the mob, won't be chatty with law enforcement. You had to know that once you were out there. Just fill me in on what you were able to find out. Especially the part about my mom dabbling in some witchcraft type stuff before coming out here to San Diego county. Also, what can you tell me about this Marco guy?"

"Okay, something tells me you want to do more than just listen to me fill you in on all that we were able to find out. I'll tell you right now, the only reason I am even allowing you to know all that we do is because you were on the inside, so to speak, and because of what you told me about your, uh, whatever it is, the ability to see victim's names on the people that killed them. If I start to see that, because it is your mom's case we're working on, it becomes too much for you, I'll make sure you stay as far away from all of it as possible. Are we clear?" Hewitt grabbed his coffee and finished off what little was left in the cup, but never looked away from Justin's face. He wanted Justin to know just how serious he was. Justin didn't have to say anything; he just nodded his head in agreement. "Now, if we're going to work together then I think we need to take our newfound teamwork into my office from here on out."

With that, they gave each other a look that confirmed without speaking that they would indeed use each other's talents, namely Justin's, in order to not only get to the bottom of his mom's murder, but maybe, just maybe, find a way to also help Detective Hewitt track down some other bad guys at the same time. They walked away from the table together, after Detective Hewitt thew down a couple of single one-dollar bills for a tip, and headed out to the parking lot. Both men were, without a doubt, trying to make sense of all the new and crazy thoughts going through their heads. For Justin, this was not exactly the way he had envisioned his new-found freedom. But, if it helped him get to the bottom of his mom's murder, then he'd work with the devil himself in order to find the people involved.

Chapter 14

Justin started the day getting prepared for his flight to Miami. He decided not to let his dad know too much of what he was planning and plotting, until he got something a little more solid to tell him. His goal was to follow as much of the trail as possible in order to make the trip out there worthwhile. Namely, find a murderer.

Detective Hewitt, knowing that Justin couldn't really pay for his own trip, had picked up the tab for his ticket simply because of his gut telling him that it'd be worth it. Maybe something right out of a science fiction movie, but what the hell? Not like he and his fellow detectives had had any luck going down the legal pathways. He told Justin to pick up a cab and meet him at the ticket counter.

Justin arrived a little early at the airport. Looking around at all the people, he was fascinated by the sheer hectic pace everyone was keeping around him. So many changes since he had been arrested and put away. Security was so intense now. More so now, he's told, due to what happened in New York on September 11, 2001. He had watched, along with the rest of the world, as the World Trade Centers came down, as well as the other attacks that had taken place. So, spending a little bit of extra time to ensure his safety was no big deal to him. This would be his first big outing since being released. Since he had discovered his "talent," or "curse" as he called it, he had been staying inside at night because he was very apprehensive about what he would see when confronted with crowds of people. What secrets would be revealed. What, and how many, skeletons would fall out of countless closets. To him, or at least in his mind, the people that he encountered, because of what he could see, didn't hide skeletons in their closets: they hid victims.

As he awaited Detective Hewitt, he took a few moments to walk over to the windows facing the plane he was about to board, and watched the airport personnel below, as they loaded the enormous amounts of baggage into it. He turned back to the sights and sounds of the gate behind him. The stagnant smell of vending machine meals. Passengers bringing along with them the smell of the several cigarettes they had inhaled in the shortest amount of time because they knew they couldn't smoke once they're waiting at the gate. Instead, they had decided to share the stench along with the non-smokers waiting with them. Thank goodness Lindbergh Field didn't have any designated smoking areas inside the terminal at all. It would for sure smell like there was a dirty ashtray inside of every air vent around. The hustle and bustle of it all was enough to make any head spin. He was enjoying it, though. Through the countless conversations going on around him, he heard his name being called out. He turned and saw the detective coming towards him.

Detective Hewitt had dressed very casually. Gray sport jacket, white t-shirt, jeans, and gray-colored hightops. Quite the contrast to Justin's black t-shirt, black hoodie, jeans, and black chucks.

"How do you like the security check here?" Detective Hewitt asked him while setting his carry-on bag on the seat next to him before sitting down.

"Pretty intense. But I understand the reason why. So, no big deal. I'm more fascinated with all the goings on around here. A person could just sit here all day and watch absolutely nothing in particular and still be entertained." Justin took a seat next to Detective Hewitt's bag before setting his carry-on bag on the floor between his legs.

"Yeah, definitely. So, when we get to Miami, we'll pick up the car rental and head over to our hotel. We'll be there early enough to meet up later with a couple of detective buddies of mine, that will help us get a short lay of the land, so to speak, before we actually dig into what we're going there for. They're the ones that led me there in the first place, and they've been super helpful."

"All this help you had, and you still couldn't find my mom's killer." Justin slumped back into his seat with his hands in the pockets of his hoodie.

"I realize it may seem that way, but until you've walked a mile in my shoes, you'll never understand. I won't pretend I know what you went through, so don't pretend to know what we didn't do for her." The detective reached into his bag for a small notepad and scribbled out the names of the two detectives they would be meeting, then tore off the little page and handed it to Justin. "These are the two we'll be working with. Maybe familiarize yourself with their names before we get there."

"Detective Bo De Silva, and Detective Paulina Ortega. Okay. Good to know. Thanks." He then stuffed the note into his front jeans pocket.

"This way you at least have their names in writing in case you forgot once I told you. They'll be meeting us tonight for dinner at the hotel. Then tomorrow we can start our digging around."

"Digging around, yeah. I'm definitely anxious about that. Hope you warned the detectives about me and my, uh, 'special' talent."

"Don't worry, I have. They're rather anxious to meet you. I have a feeling this will be a very productive trip, to say the least. It'll be interesting for sure."

"Not sure I would use the word interesting. I too have a feeling about it. My feeling, however, is more along the line of revenge. But don't worry, it'll be a lawful form of revenge. How could it not be with you around?"

Justin knew this would be a trip like no other. Hopeful would be another good word, but if he was being honest with himself, maybe the best word to describe how he felt about it would be panic. He was going to need all the patience in the world for this one. In more ways than one.

"Also, since we're going to be working with each other on this, you might as well just call me by my last name."

"Sure, okay. You got it ... uh ... Hewitt." He replied with a salute, and a wink, just as they were being called to board their flight.

Chapter 15

Arriving at the hotel, Justin was culture shocked by the vast difference not only in climate, but in the people. There was definitely a Latin flavor to everything around him. From the interior design of the furniture in the lobby, to the wall hangings. Oranges and browns just about everywhere he looked. A few splashes of neon pink to bring out the night-clubbing thoughts of some of its visitors. That was certainly one of the many things not on his mind. All he could think about was finding the killer(s) responsible for his mom not being here with him. Fun did not fit into any of it.

He and the detective checked into their respective rooms, grabbed their luggage, and rode the elevator up to the ninth floor. They had adjoining rooms, though Justin didn't think that was necessary. He unpacked his suitcase, and took in the interior of his room, as well as the view. Before he could get too lost in his thoughts, there was a knock at the door. He sure hoped the detective didn't keep using this joint door to bug him every waking moment.

He opened the door after the detective said, "It's me," loud enough for people down in the lobby to hear.

"I'm pretty sure there wouldn't be anyone else

knocking on this door, so no need to announce yourself," Justin said as he opened the door connecting their rooms.

"You never know. So, you unpacked? We can head downstairs if you're ready, and if you're hungry. De Silva and Ortega are on their way here." Hewitt sounded like and was acting like a kid in a candy store: rubbing his hands together as if he were freezing, and staring at Justin with a very wild look in his eye.

"What's got you so wound up, Hewitt?" he said as he grabbed his wallet off the dresser, along with his room key.

"I'm just happy to be out of my office for a few days, not to mention I'm starving. I'm surprised you aren't feeling the same."

"I'm hungry, yeah, just not bouncing off the walls like you are. You'd think I would be after the past fifteen years, but oddly enough, I'm just taking all of life in right now. Trying not to miss anything, I guess." He started heading to the door as Hewitt shut and locked the connecting door to their rooms. "Let's go."

They headed into a little restaurant located just off the main lobby of the hotel. As Hewitt told the cute young lady standing at the podium that they were meeting two other people, Justin looked around very cautiously, hoping he wouldn't see too much from everyone enjoying their dinners.

They were seated at a table somewhat hidden near the rear of the dimly lit eatery. Justin continued to look around, checking his surroundings, pleased to notice there were no names illuminating any of the patrons around them. That was his biggest fear. Fearful not only to have to deal with what he might see, but fearful because he didn't want his conscience to get the better of him and distract him from the real reason they were there.

Hewitt ordered himself an ice water, wanting to keep his head clear, while Justin decided to order a beer. It almost didn't matter if he kept his head clear. He'd still see what he would see no matter what. As the waitress brought their drinks, they ordered some food while waiting for the other two detectives to arrive. Hewitt ordered ceviche, while Justin ordered as simple as he could get, a Frita, a Cuban take on a burger. They asked the waitress to wait a few minutes to place their food order to allow time for the other detectives to get there.

Just after they ordered, Hewitt's cell phone went off. It was Detective De Silva. She was walking in with Detective Ortega right now. Justin suddenly became very nervous. This would be yet another first. This would be the first time he'd be in any sort of social meeting with someone of the opposite sex. Other than seeing Catherine at his place. Not that this was a social gathering to that degree, but it was still a meeting that made his heart beat a little faster, as if it wasn't beating fast enough already.

Detective Bo De Silva was introduced to Justin first

by Hewitt. Justin had expected to meet a man with that name. De Silva was about 5'8", with shoulder-length straight black hair, wearing a tan-colored button-down dress shirt, along with a mid-length black skirt and black low-heeled shoes. Ortega came in right behind her, a sharp contrast to De Silva. She was taller at about 5'10", had very short blonde hair by way of a buzz cut, and wore a black vest with no shirt underneath, paired with black jeans and Doc Marten boots. They all sat down after the introductions as the waitress walked back over with drinks. De Silva ordered a glass of water, while Ortega ordered a Pepsi, and they placed their food orders at the same time.

"Well now that we all know each other, by name anyway, let's get started with the reason we're all sitting here." Hewitt reached down and grabbed his briefcase, while the waitress brought over plates of food for everyone.

"You don't waste any time, do you, Hewitt?" said Ortega while placing a forkful of food in her mouth.

"No time like the present they say," Hewitt said before he chomped down on a forkful of food himself. He set his fork down on his plate with one hand, while placing a manila folder full of papers in the middle of the table with the other. "Thought I would refresh both your memories with the minor details of the case that has us all together like this, and also fill you in on some new details."

"You mean you've been working on this all this

time without telling us, Hewitt?" asked De Silva while reaching for a sip of her water. Ortega sat quietly while drinking her soda, and skimming through some of the reports in the folder. Justin continued to eat and drink while they all reacquainted themselves with his mom's case.

"Not exactly. There's new information that may help us get to the bottom of this case, courtesy of Justin here."

"Really?" Ortega turned to Justin while motioning to the waitress for another round. "Not finding it a bit difficult to be working on this, Justin?"

"Actually, I'm finding it helps. Besides, I want her case to finally be solved, once and for all. I'm just hoping that what I contribute accomplishes that."

As the waitress set down everyone's drinks, De Silva thought she would cut to the chase. "So, what can you contribute Justin? Let's get to the meat and potatoes of our little meeting here. What's going on, Hewitt? What's this new information, or should I say leads, that you have on this?"

"I should probably let Justin tell you," Hewitt said as he reached for his glass of water.

Justin spent the next few minutes describing what would soon be his contribution to his mother's case. Hewitt was impressed with the way he handled himself, answering all the questions thrown at him, calmly and patiently. As if he were on trial, he took his time and didn't seem to be too concerned with what they might think of him. Hewitt watched the detectives' faces as they sat through Justin's description of what he had been going through the past couple of years. He slowly explained to them that he couldn't believe what was happening to him either, and that if it was him sitting where they were now, he wouldn't even believe him. Hewitt jumped in and also explained how he put his claims to the test. After answering all of their questions as best he could, they all just sat there and let the weight of what he had just finished telling them sink in.

"So, who's ready for dessert?" asked the waitress as she broke the silence and brought De Silva and Ortega back to reality. Dessert was definitely the furthest thing from their minds.

Chapter 16

Morning brought a whole new outlook on things. Not only for Justin, but for Hewitt too. Last night's dinner was almost entertaining for him. In a sick and selfish way. He was ready to take on Carla's, or Marnie's, case as if for the first time. He told Justin he would be headed down to the local police station to speak with De Silva and Ortega first thing, very early, and that he would be back shortly after and they would get started on the reason they were there.

Hewitt drove into the parking lot of the police station, and took the first available parking spot. Arming the car, he headed inside. He had called De Silva and Ortega as he was leaving the hotel, and they told him to just let them know when he was there. As he went to the front desk sergeant, he reached for his badge and identification, and said he was expected by De Silva and Ortega. He took a seat on a nearby chair, and within three minutes was greeted by De Silva. She was wearing a navy-blue pencil skirt and a light-blue button-down shirt with a navy-blue blazer over it, her badge hanging on the waistband of the skirt.

"Thanks for meeting up with me here," Hewitt said as he shook her extended right hand.

"Of course, my pleasure. That was quite an eye-opening evening you and Justin provided me and Ortega with."

"Yeah, wasn't quite sure how you two would handle it, but seeing as you agreed to meet and discuss the case with me this morning, I guess what you heard wasn't enough to laugh us back to San Diego."

"No, as you well know, there are certain cases that go home with you, and this is one of them. So, it appears the three of us are willing to try and believe almost anything that will get us closure on it."

They walked side by side down to De Silva's office. As they stepped into it, the first thing Hewitt noticed was the much better view out of her office window than the one he had back home. Even her chairs for visitors were more comfortable.

"Please have a seat." De Silva motioned to one of those comfy-looking chairs with her left hand, while closing her office door with her right.

"Thanks. You have a very nice office here. Who is your interior designer and how much do they charge? Maybe I can hire them for mine," Hewitt said with a grin while setting his briefcase down on the floor next to him, and taking a seat across from her desk.

"Thank you. Well, the interior designer is me, and don't know if you could afford me," she replied with a snicker. "I figured since I spend way more time here than I do at home, I might as well feel like I am at home."

Hewitt chuckled back. "I can totally understand that"

"Would you like some coffee or anything? I probably should have asked before we came in here."

"No, I'm good actually. Thanks though. Had my fill already. Any more and I'll float away for sure."

She smiled back at that remark while tapping a few keys on her laptop. "So, where would you like to start? Oh, and Ortega will be joining us here shortly. She has earned enough clout around here to get a later start to her day than the rest of us." She rolled her chair a little closer to her desk, then reached for what would be her fourth cup of coffee.

"Well, good for her. I plan to do the same once I get back to San Diego. Take my time, that is. In our line of work, you know as much as I do how much of a rare commodity sleep is."

"I certainly do. So, why don't we dive into what has us up and working, before the Ortegas of the world join us." She smiled while reclining back in her chair, then folded her hands in front of her, and placed them top of her desk.

"Agreed. I brought all we have on the case. I know you spent countless hours yourself, along with Ortega, and I believe we all ended up hitting a dead end once we discovered that Carla's, or Marnie as we knew her at her death, first husband committed suicide after becoming so despondent with her leaving. Now I haven't mentioned his suicide to Justin yet. I wanted to make sure he would come out here."

"Ah. Well, I'm glad you told me that before he got here. So, we'll also need to fill him in on the fact that Marco and his family come from a long line of mafia connections, and that we were never really able to link any of those connections to Carla's, I mean ... Marnie's ...death. Our trail ended with Marco's mother paying her way to keeping us all at bay and not getting those last few leads, leading back to the family. I still believe that someone in that family is responsible, or somehow linked to those responsible for Carla's, ugh, Marnie's death. You would think I'd have remembered what to call her by now." De Silva then typed out a few things on her laptop, before reaching back to a printer behind her desk. Removing a few sheets from it, she kept a couple for herself, then reached across her desk and handed Hewitt a few copies.

"Thanks. So, what am I looking at here?" Hewitt reached out and held onto the sheets as he started reading through them.

"Well, if you recall, once you guys hit your brick wall out there in San Diego, we continued and picked up where you left off. We did manage to find a few leads, trailing back to Marco's mom, and not in a good way."

Hewitt flipped through a few sheets to the ones with Marco's mother's name on them, and started to read out loud from the first page.

"Teresa C. Jones. Born March 6th, 1936. Married to

Enzo 'The Enforcer' Florentelli from 1954 until the day Enzo passed away due to complications from liver cancer in 1969, at the young age of thirty-nine. Marco was only fifteen years old. I recall we did follow those leads back to her, but then we handed it off to you here in Florida, once we started to see that it was leading us to a possible mob connection. I assume your mob task force that you worked with took it further?" Hewitt asked as he set the pages down on his lap. As he was looking up from his copies, Detective Ortega walked through the door.

"So glad you could join us," commented De Silva with a smirk.

"This little girl enjoys her beauty sleep quite a bit, you know. Besides, helps me think clearer. Morning, Hewitt. Where's your boy with the superhero vision?" she asked as she grabbed the chair next to him and sat down.

"That's pretty good," Hewitt said with half a smile. "Don't know if he would call it that. Anyway, he's back at the hotel. Bit too early for him. Since his release he's enjoying the ability to sleep in these days."

"Ahh, yeah, I imagine he would be. Not to mention, all this newfound visionary talent of his, has to have him pretty wiped out I'm sure." She winked at Hewitt before focusing her attention on De Silva behind her desk. "So, fill me in. Better yet, just tell me where we're headed to. I'm rather eager to jumpstart this case again."

"And how many energy drinks have you had this

morning? Because I'm sure even if it was just one, that's one too many for you. I forget that you're one of those oddballs that doesn't need caffeine to keep you energized for the day, like the rest of us do," De Silva commented while reviewing some information on her laptop. "I was just about to explain to Hewitt here what we uncovered once we took the reins on the investigation."

"Fantastic! You start talking and I'll go grab some coffee. Don't worry, I'll make it decaf. I don't want to miss anything by being *too* energetic. If that's possible." With that, Ortega jumped up out of her seat and briskly headed out of the office down to the coffee machine around the corner.

"Sorry about that. I sometimes feel as though I have a teenager hyped up on an entire shipment of candy for a partner. Okay. So, I'll try to keep it short and sweet. No doubt Justin is up and getting a bit of cabin fever in his room."

"Ha! You know this is going to sound bad, but I almost forgot about him, I was so wrapped up with why we're here. I'm sure he's okay. My phone hasn't been blown up with text messages by him, so I think he's either really taking advantage of room service, or he's really taking advantage of the solitude. Maybe both. Either way, I'd like to have something new to give him about his mom's case."

"It's okay, I actually know what you mean. As for new, well, I guess it would be, wouldn't it? New for him, I mean." She picked up her copies of what she had printed out, and told Hewitt to turn to his copies, starting with page five. "Here we go."

Chapter 17

Ortega came back into the room and rejoined the conversation. Before she sat down, she was handed copies of what De Silva and Hewitt were reading. "Thanks, sure saves me the trouble of interrupting your chat. Wait, I did that anyway, didn't I, just by saying… never mind. I'm good. Carry on." She listened and caught up with them on the page showing a timeline of when Justin's mother's former in-laws met, and how the detectives believed them to be tied into her murder.

De Silva continued on. "So here is where we believe it all to have started. Teresa C. Jones meets Enzo Florentelli, they marry and have one child in 1954, Marco Romeo Florentelli. Enzo, a well-known and prominent member tied to a smaller branch of the Benorisi mob family, is happy to groom Marco to carry the torch on after he is long gone. Little does he realize that would come to fruition sooner than anticipated when he died of cancer in 1969. Teresa keeps Marco involved with the help of the rest of the mob family. Marco meets Carla in 1971, they marry in 1972. She's sixteen and a half, he is eighteen. Marco is now well versed on all that is the mob, while Carla plays the good little mob wife and doesn't question anything and is the typical stay-at-home wife."

Ortega then picked up the conversation from there. "Fast forward to around 1974, from what we gathered, Carla disappears with all that she now knows about the Benorisi family, and the mob 'doings' that Marco had tried to keep her from finding out. She somehow manages to evaporate and resurrect as Marnie Isabel Simon. Marco slips into a deep depression over her disappearance. His mom was undoubtedly at a loss as to how to help him."

"That's pretty much where we, out in San Diego, kind of hit a brick wall. We couldn't get anything beyond her disappearing from her life as Marco's wife. Which pretty much left us without those leads that would have linked him, and his mob lifestyle, to her death. So, fill me in how you may have done that for us," Hewitt said as he placed the pages he was following along with, onto De Silva's desk.

De Silva pushed back and rolled her chair away from her desk, crossing her well-toned, slender legs. "We have reason to believe that after Marco's dad, Enzo, died from cancer, combined with Carla's disappearance; his depression drove his mom Teresa, to go to extreme lengths to not only find Carla, but to make Carla pay for what she put her son through. Through a rather reliable source, we found out that Teresa used every resource of her husband's mob connection that she could, to track down Carla, now 'Marnie,' and put out an apparently successful hit on her. We discovered that there is about 5 years between the time *Carla* disappears, and *Marnie* pops up. The only trouble we have is finding the trigger man, or men. With what you and your newfound boy wonder have now brought to our table, we would like to believe that maybe there is a good chance of finding our mystery suspect and finally putting a lid on this case."

"Well, you have been busy out here. I'm just really glad to hear of all the progress you have made. And it does seem that maybe Justin will lead us to his mom's murderer. Now I believe I did also tell you that Carla, I mean Marnie, did also dabble in something related to some form of witchcraft, like spells and stuff. How that plays into all of this I don't know, but at this point I figured we need all the little tidbits of info we can get." Hewitt then stood up and laced his fingers together above his head in order to stretch. "So, if Marnie took this witchcraft stuff as seriously as we believe she did, and Justin has this... uh... gift... maybe the two of them are connected in some way."

"In what way? Like a curse or something?" Ortega said while smiling and letting out a short burst of a laugh.

"I don't know, but as far-fetched as the whole witchcraft thing is, it can't be as far-fetched as those two ideas being connected somehow. Or at the very least, we can use one or the other for some help in her unsolved case." Hewitt then crossed his arms before sitting on the edge of a small file cabinet next to De

Silva's desk.

De Silva and Ortega turned to look at each other as if saying, *'that's not a bad idea.'*

"Well then," replied De Silva while standing and placing both of her palms on the top of her desk, "I think it's time we get your *gifted* boy wonder, and at least put one of those ideas to the test, shall we?"

"I'm all for that," agreed Ortega. "So, which drive-through are we hitting on the way over?"

This time, De Silva and Hewitt were the ones staring at each other, before looking back at Ortega.

"What? All that sleep this morning made me super hungry. Besides, sounds like it's going to be a long day and I need the energy."

With that, Ortega started for the office door. De Silva and Hewitt followed right behind, but not before throwing away the super-large disposable cup of coffee that Ortega had left behind. She would for sure need food, if only to soak up all the coffee she had drunk. Not to mention energy drinks. They might all need energy drinks, or something stronger, to deal with the new direction this case was about to take. Especially if they were going to keep up with Detective Ortega.

Justin woke to voices in Hewitt's room next door. He then went over to the coffee maker, followed the instructions by placing a coffee pod inside of it, placed a disposable coffee cup below the spout under the pod, pressed the blinking blue button, and waited for it to brew. Everything now is smaller and faster, and giving him lots of new things to learn. Immediately after that, there was a knock at the adjoining doors.

"Justin, it's me, Hewitt," spoke the detective from the other side of the door.

Justin walked over to the door, unlocked and opened it for the good detective, then walked back over to the coffeemaker. While lifting the cup up and preparing to take his first sip of it, he turned to Hewitt, "Well, I sure didn't think you were room service." Hewitt followed him over to the small sofa and sat at the end closest to the window, while Justin took a seat at the little table next to the same window. "Help yourself to some coffee," he said to Hewitt.

"I'm actually good, thanks. I've been up for the past four hours, talking things over with Ortega and De Silva. Figured we'd let you sleep in while we discussed, and combine our information about your mom's case. They're in my room, they should be in here any ..."

"Do I smell coffee?" said Ortega as she walked into the room, followed closely behind by De Silva.

"I definitely don't think you need any more coffee," stated De Silva. "Good morning, Justin. Or should I say, good afternoon. Hope you had a good night's sleep."

"I did, thanks," he replied with a smile, then took another sip of coffee.

"Listen." Hewitt starts the conversation going. "Have something to tell you that I hesitated in telling you sooner because I just needed to sort things out about you, and how we were going to proceed." That left everyone just staying quiet while he spoke first. "Marco is dead. He committed suicide. In 2009." Hewitt let that sink in with Justin before moving on.

Justin just stared blankly at him, and then the other two detectives. "2009?!" He answered back, raising his voice slightly. "What? And you just wanted to keep that from me, why, because you thought I wouldn't come out here with you or something?!"

"I believe Hewitt was just wanting to make sure we had everything prepared before you both made the trip out here, and didn't want to feel like this would be a waste of your time."

"Great! So now what?" He sits with his arms crossed, paired with a frown on his face. Like a child internalizing a temper tantrum.

"So, we have a couple of ideas, on how we can all work together and make some headway on your mom's case. Now, I know you're as anxious as we are, and you want to dive right into everything, but we need to make sure that we stick close to the evidence and follow where it leads us. Because you came to me for help, convinced me to work the case again, and since I've now convinced Detectives Ortega, and De Silva, to agree to help us, I want to make sure you agree to let us do this the right way. Without you getting too excited and going off on your own at any time, okay?" Hewitt said while staring Justin dead in the eyes. He then glanced over at Ortega and De Silva. They both nodded at him in agreement, then all eyes were on Justin again.

"No need to get so serious, dude. I'm all about doing things the 'legal' way now," Justin replied by motioning with air quotes when saying the word legal. "I'll be a good boy and follow orders, don't worry." With that, he stood up and threw away his disposable coffee cup. He then started to take off his sweat pants, much to the astonishment of the detectives. "You all going to stand around here and watch me get naked or do I actually have to get dressed in the bathroom?"

With that, the three detectives gladly made their way back into Hewitt's room and waited for Justin to finish getting dressed.

"I forget that he is probably used to getting dressed in front of other people, no matter who it is," said De Silva.

"Yeah, well, I'm just glad he stopped before completely removing his sweats," Ortega said with a laugh.

"And I'm just glad he had boxers on underneath them," responded Hewitt. They all sat and gathered their thoughts as they prepared for the roller coaster, they were all about to take a ride on. Though Hewitt really stressed to Justin the fact this all had to go by the book, he, and maybe the other two detectives as well, knew damn well that more than half of what they were about to embark on wouldn't be in any book. Legal or otherwise. He just hoped that this roller coaster ride actually did come to a proper stop, and not fly off its track… and end up with them all six feet under as a result.

Chapter 18

On their way to their first stop, Detective Hewitt filled Justin in with a very short, summarized story about the Florentelli family, their mob connections, and how they believed Mrs. Florentelli might be tied to his mother's death.

"So, if I'm to believe what you're telling me, my mom Marnie, I mean, 'Carla,' is dead because of a hit that was put on her by her own mother-in-law?" Justin said to Hewitt with a furrowed brow. De Silva glanced into the rear-view mirror back at Justin, then over at Hewitt. Ortega glanced over at De Silva from the front passenger seat, while De Silva was steering them down the South Beach Miami main street of Ocean Drive.

"That's our theory. That's what we believe happened. I couldn't get far enough with the evidence I had to get a solid link back to her, mainly because I kept hitting brick walls most likely placed there, theoretically anyway, by the mob themselves. Detectives De Silva and Ortega, however, got much farther than I did, and even though they did, they still had trouble being handed to them courtesy of the mob as well."

De Silva chimed in from behind the wheel, "If what you can bring to the table leads us further past those brick walls that the mob put up, then we know for certain that we can get to the bottom of this, and bring whoever did this to justice."

"Okay," replied Justin, staring back and forth between De Silva and Ortega. "So, where are we going now then?"

"We are going to go pay a visit to Teresa Jones-Florentelli. Which in and of itself was quite a feat to set up, I must say," answered Ortega. "She didn't exactly appreciate being bothered while in the middle of, more than likely, doing nothing. In her sprawling twenty thousand plus square foot of a home. In one of the most expensive areas of Miami. Who needs seven bedrooms anyway?" she said. "Not only that, the house was something like thirty million dollars. Just an insane amount. But, when you are tied in with the mob, you can live very nicely. It's definitely *way* beyond my budget. I'm happy to be on my beer budget myself."

"And does she know anything about me right now? Because if so, I don't want anything happening to my dad back home. If she's responsible for my mom's death, I don't want her taking him too"

"No, she doesn't, and we'd like to keep it that way. Don't worry about your dad. We will make sure she knows little to nothing about you or him," Hewitt said to him as they were getting ready to drive up to the gates of the sprawling mansion of a home.

De Silva drove into the driveway and stopped the car about thirty yards in front of black iron gates. She pushed the button on her door panel to bring her window down, and reached out to press the intercom button. Justin immediately tensed up, while the other detectives seemed to be rather cool about the whole thing. He knew they had to be accustomed to this type of scenario. He watched the black iron monster gates slowly swing open inwards toward the incredibly long drive to the front door. The home itself seemed so small from the gates, but up close was absolutely massive. It looked like something right out of a scene from *Gone with the Wind*. The pillars were monstrous. De Silva drove up as close as she could get the car to the front door. There were two men in dark suits standing on either side of the huge front doors. The suits walked down the stairs towards them, and with one on either side of the car, they opened the driver and passenger doors on both sides of the car. Before they all stepped out of the car, Detective Hewitt looked at him and said, "Just stick close to me, let us do all the talking, and if you by any chance see or hear anything that is out of the norm, let us know when we leave, okay?"

"Don't worry, I'm just along for the ride right now. If I do see or hear something, I won't have to tell you. You'll see it on my face. I just hope I won't be read like a book if that does happen, though." With that, everyone stepped out of the car, and Justin thought for sure everyone around him could hear his heart beating out of his chest. Time to test his skills, if that was what he wanted to call it.

Chapter 19

The four of them walked into a grander than grand, foyer. Justin had never seen so much marble in his life. Floors, pillars, tables, all marble. As he stared straight ahead, there was a wall of nothing but windows, with French doors leading out to the impeccably landscaped backyard with waterfalls spilling into a swimming pool large enough for any Olympic trial. Palm trees lined the edges of the yard. They were all led into a sitting room off to the right of the living room.

"Mrs. Florentelli will be with you momentarily. May I get anyone a beverage?" said a middle-aged woman aptly outfitted in a typical maid's uniform.

"I'll have a beer, doesn't matter what kind," Ortega snickered. That drew a sideways glance from the rest of them. "Just kidding, make that a cup of decaf coffee, please." She then got comfortable in a red leather chair big enough for two people. Justin sat himself down in a duplicate chair across from Ortega. Hewitt and De Silva sat themselves on opposite ends of a red leather sofa. The housekeeper, then seeing that Ortega was the only one thirsty, disappeared down a hallway in order to get her coffee.

De Silva looked over at Ortega, took a short pause

then said, "I'm glad you changed your choice of beverage. We are on the clock after all. We all have to pay close attention to everything Mrs. Florentelli says, and how she says it. Mannerisms. All of it."

"Isn't she going to be a curious with why I'm here? Let alone wonder who the hell I am?" asked Justin, concerned that his being there might ruin their visit.

"Today you are my younger brother. And it will actually help, I hope, because it will give her the sense of this visit being nothing as official as she may think it is. Just observe. We'll take care of the rest," Hewitt spoke softly to Justin.

Shortly after speaking those words, walked in an elderly, slightly overweight, well-dressed woman. She had wavy, mid-length, all white hair. Gold teardrop style earrings. A black, very smart and classy looking pant suit. She topped it off with an off-white scarf. They all stood up when she walked in the room.

"Please, have a seat," she stated to them, and they took their seats again. Right behind her, was her housekeeper with a tray containing a pitcher of ice water, four glasses, along with a small carafe of coffee, and one cup. She poured the coffee into the cup, and handed it to Ortega. She then turned to Mrs. Florentelli and asked her what she would like to drink. "Just bring me some iced tea, Marta, thank you." With that, Marta set the tray on a coffee table between everyone, and walked back down the hallway, back in the direction of what must be the kitchen.

"Thank you for agreeing to meet with us, Mrs. Florentelli," said De Silva first.

"Of course, detective. I must say I was somewhat surprised to hear from you again. But a pleasure to see you in any case. Good to see you again Detective… ummm… Ortega, correct?"

"Yes, correct. Nice to see you again as well ma'am."

"And though I do recognize you, forgive me if I don't remember your name." She said while looking at Detective Hewitt.

"It's quite all right. We didn't see each other quite as often as you saw my two lovely associates. I'm Detective Hewitt from San Diego." He half stood and reached over to her to shake her hand. "This is my brother Justin. He's on vacation out here. We thought we would tag along with the good detectives here. Hope you don't mind the intrusion." Justin did the same and reached over to shake her hand as well.

"Not at all. It's nice to see you again as well. And a pleasure to meet you, Justin."

Marta walked in with a smaller tray, one that only had a glass of iced tea, a small dish with lemon wedges, a few packets of artificial sweetener, and a small bowl with ice cubes and tongs. After setting the tray down on the coffee table between them all, Marta then disappeared again to the kitchen.

"So, detectives," she said as she reached for her tea, "to what do I owe this pleasant reunion of sorts to?"

"Well, if you recall, we were investigating the missing person's case, which then turned into the homicide, of your daughter-in-law Carla…"

"Ex-daughter-in-law Carla." Teresa says, interrupting her.

"I just meant that at the time of her disappearance, she and your son Marco were still married. But yes, forgive me, your ex-daughter-in-law," continued De Silva. "We wanted to let you know that we are once again reviewing her case due to some new evidence that has surfaced." She let that just float in the air between them for a few moments. "If you recall at the time, we had reason to believe that we had the right suspect in our sights. That suspect, if you also recall, was an associate of your son Marco, but we were never able to gather enough evidence to garner an arrest of the person who we believe may have been responsible, due to the untimely passing of Marco. We do know he took his life about six years ago, of which we are sincerely sorry for your loss."

"Yes. He did." She very sternly replied. "And what, pray tell, does your new evidence have to do with me?" she asked, while lifting the glass of iced tea to her mouth.

Detective Ortega then spoke up. "Well, this new evidence is once again bringing us back to one of the associates that worked closely with your son. Since we of course are unable to discuss anything about this with him, we wanted to at least let you know that we'll be working on it, and with your permission we'd like to come to you for help if need be."

Mrs. Florentelli had a fantastic poker face, because there was no way to tell how what she just heard made her feel. The detectives had hoped they'd be able to see a reaction. A flinch. Anything. All they got, though, was a solemn look.

She then took a deep breath, and let it out slowly before speaking. "And as *you'll* recall, you know what I've always believed to be true. That had it not been for her little disappearing act, my Marco would still be alive today. So, forgive me if I'm not anxious to help you in your newfound direction in the investigation." The detectives all gave a solemn eye to one another. "My son adored her, gave her anything and everything she could ever want. For what? For him to have it all basically thrown back in his face, as if nothing was ever good enough for her?" She then stood up, and walked over to the fireplace mantle a few feet away. Staring into a photo of her son she continued, with her back to them all, she continued on. "Did you know, detectives, that Carla's parents practically forced Marco and her together? That they couldn't give their blessing fast enough for their sixteen-and-a-half-year-old daughter. No doubt because they knew she would be well taken care of. Marco didn't have to ask for their blessing, but we raised him to be a good man, and since she was so young he also knew he had to. He was eighteen-years old; we provided a good life for him. He didn't have to work. His father left him with the knowledge to not have to work, and enjoy his young life, before he passed away. Marco became a man very quickly, and was financially set for life. He just couldn't wait to share it with her."

The detectives looked back and forth between themselves, before re-focusing their attention to the broken woman in front of the fireplace. Justin looked over at Hewitt as if to say, "What the hell is she talking about?" Hewitt just gave him a look that told him to just stay quiet.

Mrs. Florentelli slowly turned around, she walked back to her seat, along with the photo of Marco, and placed it on the coffee table facing her. "Her parents were barely getting by with only her dad working, so when Marco told them that he would take care of everything Carla would ever want, and need, they of course jumped at their good fortune. It was almost as if they were dating Marco. He swore to them that she would have the best education, a roof over her head always, and she would never have to want for anything."

"No, we didn't know that." Hewitt said.

"No, of course you didn't. That's because all you detectives cared about was looking for every opportunity you could to dig up some dirt on my family. Using whatever you could find to try and link her death to us however you could. Never could though, could you? Now you want me to help you? Well, that's rich, isn't it?"

"Mrs. Florentelli, we understand your reluctance to help out." De Silva tried to turn the conversation around from a direction she didn't want it to take. "I know it may have appeared that our investigation was anything other than finding out who killed Carla, but that is, and always has been our goal. We never meant for Marco to take his own life over her death, nor did we ever intend to slander your family's name at all. We regretted putting you and your family through all of that. We hope you believe that."

"What I believe is that you're saying that just to get my help."

"I assure you it isn't. Truly." Ortega said with as much sincerity as one could muster. "Is there something that you can help us out with that maybe might have slipped your mind when we first started our investigation?" She asked.

"Of course not, and I do believe we've discussed this more than I care to. So, I think it best you all leave now."

They all just sat quietly, and exchanged quick glances at each other. All of them somewhat expecting that their departure would be done in a quick manner.

"Of course. We understand. We've taken up enough of your time." Hewitt said as he stood up first.

"Thank you for your hospitality, Mrs. Florentelli, it was very nice to meet you." Justin was somewhat confused and anxious to find out what he had just witnessed in such a short amount of time.

"We'll see ourselves out. But I do hope that we can contact you if we need any further information." De Silva was the last one to start towards the door.

Mrs. Florentelli stood and took a few steps towards De Silva. "You go ahead and call. I can't say I'll be able to help, especially since we didn't seem to have the kind of help my Marco needed in finding her back then. But you call."

They all left without saying a word to each other. Feeling slightly defeated from the short visit. Once they were all in the car, Justin sat and stared around the car and realized that if thoughts could make noise, the sound would be deafening right about now.

Chapter 20

"So, who wants to fill in the gaps for me?" Justin broke the silence first as they drove away.

"The gaps are, your mother did what she thought she needed to do in order to escape a husband that she felt misled her, ignored her, lied to her, and all around betrayed her with his secret Mafia lifestyle, but yes, we'll go through what we believe to be the timeline with you later." Ortega spoke from behind the wheel. "What you heard back there was a mother who is still grieving, but also in denial about what her family lifestyle really is, or was about, back then. Your mother was young, naïve, and ultimately betrayed by her parents first, then by Marco. She probably felt as though she had no other option but to disappear."

"And did you guys help them by trying to find her? Or did you not make much of an effort because of who they were?"

"We did as much as we could, with the information and resources we had." De Silva said from the passenger seat.

"From the way Mrs. Florentelli spoke, you'd think that…" he stopped talking as he saw a man walking on the side of the road wearing a tank top, and jeans, along with two other men that made him whip his head around and look out the rear window of the car in order to continue looking at that man. What he saw was a glow in the form of a name coming from the man's shoulder. It was exactly what he had dreaded seeing once he had learned about his ability to do so. A name, a light, a beacon spotlighting someone that decided they would be judge and jury for whatever reason in snuffing out a life.

"Justin, what is it?" Hewitt looked in the direction he was looking. Hewitt was looking at the same group of men walking, and didn't see anything out of the ordinary.

"The man in the white tank top, walking ahead of everyone else, killed someone. I didn't see the date clearly, but I did see the name. MaryAnn. I didn't get to see the last name because we're in a moving car. But I did see the first name pretty clearly. MaryAnn. Not two separate words, all one word. This is so crazy. This is the first time I've seen this happen outside of prison… it's pretty surreal. Should we do something?"

"I thought you were only able to see names at night?"

"Me too. Apparently not." Justin confirmed.

"My initial reaction would be to absolutely do something," Ortega said while checking her rear-view window. "However, if we just start grabbing all the people you see names on, and have nothing to back it up with, other than your word, we'll be in a world of trouble and be laughed out of every D.A.'s office, as well as any courtroom... even if we were to make it into a courtroom."

"She's right, Justin." De Silva turned around, and responded back, while looking out the window over Justin's shoulder. "I know it's going to be difficult for you to not do anything about it, but you'll have to really work hard on restraining yourself. Especially if you're with us when this is happening. I should say, more so when you're not with us. We don't want you putting yourself back in prison again. You'll be no good to not only us, but to yourself. To your father. And more importantly to getting justice for your mother."

"I know. I will." Justin tried to put what he just saw out of his mind. "So where to? Where do we start?"

"We go speak to someone that was a former known associate that we only recently were able to find a little more dirt on. He came forward on his own because he said the guilt was killing him. We had him on our radar, but could never get those leads to get us as far as we had hoped." Ortega said, while they continued to drive through what seemed to be a very decent neighborhood.

"In case I didn't mention it before, this was the first big case for both my fellow detectives here. Right after making rank. All this before age thirty-five. And it's been a fun one so far." He said to Justin. "So, who is this person, and how are they connected to the Florentellis?" asked Hewitt from the back seat.

"Yeah, we're pretty proud of ourselves too. I

wouldn't call this case fun though." De Silva said with a smile. "So, this guy isn't exactly connected to them in the way we consider someone to be connected. He's a cab driver. One who was used quite frequently in driving Marco to a variety of meetings. Marco would use this man in lieu of his own personal driver, just to mix things up a bit, and in case he was being followed at all."

"I'm assuming he was undoubtedly privy to a lot of conversations."

"Yes, he was. Marco of course used a lot of threats, and strong armed him into keeping quiet about anything he may have heard. Fortunately for us, Marco's tactics in using him to confuse us didn't work very well. Obviously. We thought we'd catch Marco using a credit card somewhere, while we were tailing him shortly after Carla disappeared, back in 2007, but he continued to use cash, except for the one time he didn't. This was some thirty plus years after your mom disappeared from Marco's life. That's how we found out about our friend the cab driver. The only thing was, that we could never get him to talk. We continued to keep a light eye on him, hoping he would do something that we could use as leverage, to get him to talk to us about Marco." Ortega drove them up to a house, that was set quite a way back from the street. Nothing like the mansion they had just left. There was a front lawn that was in desperate need of some attention, as it was scattered with a variety of brown patches, likely where green grass used to be. As well as the obligatory bicycle laying on its side in the middle of the driveway. No sight of any car sitting in the driveway with the bike, but there were a couple of newspapers wrapped in plastic thrown down here and there.

"Marco killed himself in 2009, and we didn't have our leverage against our boy here, until recently," Ortega explained while checking herself in the mirror that was on the other side of the visor. "In Dade County, where our boy here drives his cab, cab drivers can add on a per-trip fuel surcharge to fairs, if the cost of gasoline rises to a determined amount. Well, our boy here…"

"Does 'your boy' have a name? I don't want to go in there and refer to him only as *your boy*." Justin let his frustration be known.

"Rudy, his name is Rudy. Sorry about that. So, anyway. Rudy had always been our only real way of getting anything on Marco, and hopefully, those responsible for Carla's death. But he'd been keeping the straight and narrow until we noticed he was fudging the numbers on his fuel surcharges. We figured that would be the only way we could catch him on something that should be legally reported, and him forgetting that it is. In other words, he isn't the sharpest knife in the drawer and didn't think he would be caught. So, we finally had our leverage, and once Hewitt told us about your visit to him, we sat on this latest information 'til we got you both out here and meet with you, face-to-face."

"So, what are we waiting for? Let's go talk to him." Justin took off his seatbelt and started to get out from the back seat.

"Justin, wait!" The detectives all tried to catch him before he jumped out and approached the front door of the house.

They weren't fast enough as he rang the doorbell, and knocked at the front door to a nice-looking stucco-faced, brown-colored condominium. Decent looking place for a cab driver's salary. Small potted flowers lined the stairs leading to the door. They waited and listened to locks being disengaged. Justin was at the top of the stairs, with Hewitt right behind him, and De Silva and Ortega standing next to each other on the sidewalk leading up to the stairs.

"Hewitt you need to reel him in or I will." De Silva said with look that would melt metal. "Justin, you need to let me get up there. Rudy doesn't know you."

Hewitt pulled back on Justin's arm to make him step down.

"I will make him know me, and besides, you're only a couple feet away from the door. So, it's not like he won't see or recognize you." Justin complained.

She ignored what he said and stepped up the stairs to stand in front of him.

The door opened to a middle-aged woman, drying her hands off on a dish towel.

"Can I help you?"

De Silva flashed her detective badge at her while

introducing herself. "Good afternoon, ma'am. My name is Detective Bo De Silva with Miami-Dade Police Department's Homicide Division. This is my partner Detective Ortega, Detective Hewitt with San Diego Police Department, and this is Mr. Justin Ancin. We're looking to speak with Rudy Falcone. Is he here?"

"What's this about? I'm his girlfriend, Anna, and he won't be home for another thirty minutes or so."

"I'm afraid I'm not at liberty to discuss why. We just have a few questions for him about a case we're working on. If you don't mind, we'd appreciate if you let us wait for him. May we come in?"

"Do you have a warrant?"

"We won't be performing any property searches, ma'am. Just have a few questions for him is all. If you'd rather we wait out here, that's fine."

"No... no... I guess it's okay. You can come in." She stepped aside and pulled the door with her, allowing them to step inside. "Have a seat. Since you're going to be waiting a few minutes, can I get anyone something to drink?"

"Just water for me, thank you." De Silva said while taking a seat on a leather sofa. Ortega took a seat next to her, as well as Justin.

"Water sounds fine, thanks." Justin replied. Wondering why would anyone want leather furniture, in this kind of climate. Something he noted at the home they had just left as well. Nothing like sitting down, and getting stuck to the furniture if you didn't have pants on.

"I'm good, thank you, anyway." Hewitt was last to speak. He didn't sit, instead choosing to walk around the living room to look at some pictures that were on display.

While waiting, Ortega was looking around as well from her seat.

"Hey, Hewitt, check out that pic in the corner over there." She said softly.

Hewitt looked over at the little corner table where there was a small 4" x 5" photo of two men together.

De Silva confirms that the man with Rudy is Marco.

"I'm thinking that Rudy still thinks pretty highly of Marco. Anyone that has a photo of themselves with someone that is dead must miss them. And if they miss that person, maybe that'll give us a slight advantage in playing on their sympathies a little. Well, that and the other slight advantage we have with regards to his shady cab doings."

"Yeah, well, we'll find out soon enough just how sympathetic ol' Rudy is. Won't we? Sooner than we think because I believe I see him driving up as we speak." Ortega mentions, causing them all to look at the front living room window. "He may be the one needing the water that Anna is about to bring out. Something tells me his mouth may soon get a bit dry."

Chapter 21

Anna walked back into the living room carrying a tray of ice water. As she set it down, she turned around to the sound of the front door opening as Rudy was walking in. She started walking toward him as he was closing and locking the front door. Rudy stood near the entry way to where the detectives were sitting. He frowned as he stared at them all, then stared back at Anna.

"What's going on here?" he asked as she placed her arms around his waist and kissed his cheek. He looked past her face to the four people in his living room.

"They're detectives, here to ask you some questions. I asked them for a warrant, but they said they didn't need one if they were just here to talk to you. Rudy, what's going on? Why are they here? Are you in some sort of trouble…? Is there…?" She nervously said to him, before he made his way to their guests.

"It's okay, babe." Rudy kissed her forehead, while staring into the room that now had four pairs of eyes on him. "Don't worry. I'll handle this. Do me a favor will ya, and get me a beer?" Anna glanced towards the detectives and then back to Rudy. "Sure, baby." Anna gave a quick side glance to everyone now standing, then walked towards the kitchen.

He watched Anna walk into the kitchen, while he made his way over to the unexpected company in his living room. "Detectives. Can't say it's a pleasure to see you again. And I see you brought some unfamiliar faces with you to this little unscheduled reunion."

"Hi Rudy," De Silva said while walking towards him, and extending her right hand to shake his hand. "It's been a while, hasn't it?"

"Clearly not long enough. So, what's this about? Detective Ortega. Long time no see. Who are your other players here?"

"Hi, I'm Detective Hewitt from San Diego, and this is Justin Ancin." The men all shook hands before sitting down.

"Nice to meet you. So, what gives. What's this all about?" He replies while getting comfortable on the sofa, making some room for Anna as she returns with his drink from the kitchen. Feeling his neck tighten from the blood pressure now rising. Physical evidence that his nerves are starting to get the better of him. Small beads of sweat began to form at his hairline, while his palms started to match, with moisture of their own, signs of news he isn't prepared for. Handing him his beer, Anna takes a seat next to him while staring intently into his eyes.

"We have a few questions for you. Are you all right with us talking freely in front of Anna?" Ortega asked.

"Yeah, sure. I have nothing to hide."

"Funny you should say that. Because something tells me you've been doing just that all along." Ortega watched as the look of sheer confusion washed over Anna's face.

Rudy looked at Anna and held her hand in his lap. "Rudy, what did you do?"

"I didn't do anything. But I am sorry for whatever you're about to hear."

"C'mon Rudy. Why the doom and gloom? It's not too bad." De Silva stood up while continuing to talk. "Well, I guess it could be. We'd like to talk to you about your fares, and the 'fees' you've been charging them. Or should I say overcharging them? We know about your fuel surcharges, and that you've been taking real advantage of that for your benefit. When we last spoke to you, it had to do with some of the conversations you overheard while driving Marco Florentelli around. We know, from what you've told us, that he trusted you enough to be comfortable in discussing his many 'business' doings in your presence."

"So, I padded my surcharges a bit, so what? Just about every cab driver I know does that. What's that got to do with whatever I overheard Marco talk about?"

"Well, what it has to do with those conversations is that we didn't really have the authority until recently to even find out that you did that. And now that we know, we'd like to know more about those little conversations."

"And what makes you think that I'll tell you

anything about those talks I overheard? Or that I'd even be telling you the truth?"

"Well, we believe you'll be pretty truthful with us." This time Hewitt was doing the talking.

Rudy turned and faced Hewitt. "And what exactly do you have to do, with any of this, mister detective man? Let alone your sidekick there?"

"No need to be rude there, Rudy. We just..."

"It's okay, Detective Ortega, I got this. After all, we are unexpected guests in his house."

"Yeah, you sure as hell are," Rudy said rather gruffly while standing up and walking towards Hewitt.

"Okay, okay, calm down Rudy." Hewitt said while holding his hands up with his palms facing Rudy. The other two detectives stand up in defense, as Rudy backs up and heads back to sit down. "Listen," Hewitt continues on, as everyone sits back in their seat, "I have re-visited a case of mine. It's of a homicide victim by the name of Marnie Isabel Ancin, Justin here is her son."

Rudy turned and looked at Justin. "Sorry for your loss, kid." He continues to stare down the detectives while saying, "but what does that have to do with me? I don't know who you're talking about."

"Marnie's real name was Carla Rose Florentelli. Marco's wife," De Silva relayed to Rudy.

"Marco's wife? His wife disappeared years ago... wait a minute... you don't think that I..." His voice trailed off slowly while he slowly stood up again, he took his gaze from one detective to the next. "You think that some of the conversations I overheard Marco having, may have had something to do with her disappearance? And now you're talking murder? Carla's murder?"

"We want to believe that you weren't involved in any way. While we do believe you weren't, we suspect there may have been some names in those conversations that we could investigate, which may help lead us to her killer, or killers." Ortega then took a sip of water.

"What's in this for me? I mean, if I help you with some names, what do I get out of all of this?"

"You mean besides knowing you'd be helping out and doing the right thing?" De Silva chimed in. Rudy looked away and stared down at his feet.

"I for one will be grateful if it helps lead the detectives here in the right direction. I mean, I know you don't know me and have no real reason to help me, but if it were your mom, you'd want some help, wouldn't you?" Justin kept his plea short and sweet and kept his eyes staring dead center into Rudy's.

De Silva watched for Rudy's reaction to Justin's subtle plea, before saying anything further.

"Okay, so, how about this, Rudy? If your help gets us closer to who we are looking for, then we will do what we can to make sure any judge goes easy and light on your charges… about the surcharges." De Silva was not one to make promises she couldn't keep, but felt she'd be able to keep this one.

Rudy let out a big sigh before looking at Anna,

taking her hand in his again he looked back at the detectives and said, "Fine... how many names you want?"

With that, Ortega and De Silva each took out a small notepad from an inner pocket of their jackets and prepared to start writing.

Chapter 22

Rudy stood up and walked over to a bookshelf that stood against a wall at the end of a small hallway. He pulled out a book that had some pages torn out and were replaced with his own small folded-up pieces of paper. He had been keeping the names of certain individuals that he had overheard Marco mention, memorized, then wrote them down just in case he ever needed them. He was never sure why he kept the names, but apparently, this was the moment that was meant to happen.

He walked back into the room, and handed his notes with a few scribbled names on them over to De Silva. "I honestly don't know why I felt I needed to pay attention to the people he was talking about. I guess I must have figured he would have taken care of the surcharges for me. Sort of like his way of showing how much he appreciated my driving him around without any questions. Apparently, my subconscious knew him well enough to know I needed to keep track of those names. Otherwise, you probably wouldn't be here right now." De Silva opened up the folded notes, and started to review the small list of names. While looking them over, Ortega leaned over to peek over her shoulders at the names.

Hewitt glanced once at Rudy, then kept his eyes on Justin. Justin had a somewhat anxious look to him. He was rubbing his hands together, as if they were cold. He couldn't even imagine what might be going through Justin's mind right now. No doubt, what must be the only real concrete thought in his mind right now was finding his mother's killer. Whether that killer's name was on that small sheet of paper or not, at least it was more than what the two of them had when they left San Diego.

Rudy stood next to where Anna was sitting and placed his hands in his pockets.

"I count about six names on this little makeshift list of yours, Rudy. Anybody else you feel you need to add?" De Silva folded it back up and placed it in an inside coat pocket of hers while staring at Rudy. "I can keep this right?"

Rudy lets out a long sigh before answering, "Yeah, go ahead. And no, those were the only ones he ever mentioned in the car, or while he was on his cell phone. He always asked me if he could trust me, and I of course said he could. I didn't think I would ever betray that trust."

"You knew you would, otherwise you wouldn't have written those names down." Ortega says to him. "Your gut knew you would betray him, even if you didn't. But if you look at this as not so much as a betrayal, but as doing the right thing, then that should make it a little easier to swallow."

"Yeah, well, no matter how I look at it, it's still a betrayal. Marco was very generous. He paid me good money."

"Well, some of that 'generosity' was earned in a decent way. The rest of it, not so much. You knew his family, right? As far as how they came to be as prominent as they were?"

"Of course, I did. But, once you are in their good graces, you do everything you can to stay there."

"Yeah, we hear you." De Silva started to stand and make her way towards the front door. As she did, Justin stood up and started to walk slowly behind her, as did Hewitt and Ortega.

"We appreciate you allowing us to talk with you, and we really appreciate you giving us this information. You won't be needing it anymore, will you?"

Rudy just nodded. "That's it? Now what? You going to help me with those surcharges now?"

"We'll be in touch. Don't worry. What we'd also appreciate is not discussing our visit here with anyone. That will help us keep our word on helping you, with those surcharges. But, so long as we can trust you to not speak to anyone about us, then you'll just have to trust us as well. That way we can reach out to our friends, the judges. I know you understand." Rudy nodded his head up and down as Ortega walked over and reached out to shake his hand, then Anna's. "Thanks for taking time to talk to us. Nice meeting you and we will be in touch for sure. Thanks for the water."

The other detectives, and Justin, followed suit and all shook hands with him, and Anna. "We'll see ourselves out. Thanks again." Hewitt led the way to the door as he held it open for Justin and the detectives. Before he closed the door, Rudy called his name. "So, Detective Hewitt, listen, I've been on the straight and narrow here since Marco died you know? His family pretty much tossed me aside since there wasn't anyone that needed any of my services any more. I honestly haven't done anything to pad my surcharges since then, I swear. Could you please mention that to Detectives De Silva and Ortega for me? I want to continue building my life here with Anna and I don't want to get into any trouble, you know? I didn't tell her everything. She knew I was a driver for Marco, but she thought that was all it was, you know? She's a bit naïve when it comes to the whole mobster type of living that he was involved in. If she knew I was quiet about anything that I shouldn't have been then... well... I just don't want to lose her trust in me, you know? I'll tell her as much as she needs to know without completely blowing things for her and I, you know? I want to do the right thing, Detective, I truly do. I'm trying here."

Hewitt watched as Ortega, and Justin get into the car. De Silva sensed something was happening so she stood outside of the car watching him talk to Rudy. Hewitt stared at De Silva for a few more seconds and gave a long blink of his eyes to let her know everything was okay, before giving Rudy his attention again.

"We're just trying to get to the bottom of all of this, Rudy. We know you're not involved, and we can clearly see that you are doing all you can to build yourself a good life here. Anna seems like a sweet woman, and I'm sure you want to do right by her, too. I know you and I haven't dealt with each other as much as you have with Detectives Ortega and De Silva, but I give you my word we'll do what we can for you in return for your help, okay?" He shook his hand again, then patted Rudy's shoulder before walking towards the car.

"Thanks, Detective, I appreciate it."

As they began to drive away, Justin looked out of his window and continued to stare at Rudy's home. He felt a sudden flush of warmth wash over his face, and his body. Almost like a sense of relief. Practically as warm as a hug. Something tells him that this short meeting with Rudy was exactly what needed to happen. A meeting set in motion to find his mother's killer. Always a believer that everything happens for a reason, good or bad, he knew in his gut that everything up to this moment, to this point, had to happen. He was exactly where he needed to be. He also knew that though he and his dad hadn't spent much time with each other, that would happen, in time. This meeting helped bring that time closer to them both. Something also told him that one of those names on the little list that De Silva now had in her pocket belonged to exactly who they are looking for. Now, all they needed to do was just find the person belonging to that name. With whatever guidance and help, supernatural or otherwise, Justin knew, without any doubt in his mind or heart, that they would.

Chapter 23

Detective De Silva parked, and everyone slowly got out of the car. Not much was said by anyone on the way back to the station. One could almost hear everyone's wheels turning in their heads. Hard to say who had the most to think about. All three detectives undoubtedly would have been thinking very similar thoughts. Plotting their next move. Their next possible suspect. Who to call, visit, interrogate? Knowing they would have to be careful, because most certainly all those names must know each other, or at the very least, of each other. So, they'd have to be very careful not to tip one or the other off, and have them all scatter like a bunch of cockroaches after a light is switched on. The actions of timing and planning are often strange bedfellows, but, if approached in the proper sequence, can work.

Justin spoke first as they made their way up the stairs to the entrance. "So now what?"

"Now," De Silva chimed in, "we split up these names between the three of us, make a few phone calls, track them down, set up a couple meetings. Basically, shake the proverbial trees and see what falls."

"Well, that's great for the three of you, what do I

get to do?"

"You can sit tight back at the hotel. We are used to burning the midnight oil, so given that it is getting a bit late you can go chill for now while we lay the groundwork on how to proceed from here."

"I don't want to sound ungrateful here, because I do appreciate all you guys are doing to help me out, but I haven't done anything yet, at all. So, if anyone is somewhat rested due to not doing much of anything, and able to really burn that midnight oil, it's me. Give me something to do, otherwise I'll go stir-crazy in my room and will want to do nothing but wander around this place and play tourist. And to be perfectly honest with you, I really don't want to see what I may see without you guys around, if you know what I mean."

The detectives exchanged looks between each other before anyone said anything.

"I wouldn't say you haven't done anything at all Justin. Speaking for myself, if you hadn't come to me back in San Diego shortly after your release, we more than likely wouldn't be here discussing what to do next," Hewitt said while holding the door open for everyone. "Thanks to you, hopefully we can work on bringing both your mom, and her killer, some justice."

"Okay, so can I just hang out with you guys while you start setting up your game plan here?"

They again all exchanged looks with one another.

"I don't see why you can't just hang back with us, so long as you don't get in the way here. May take us a while to figure out our next move, or moves," Ortega said as she walked ahead of everyone on her way to De Silva's office. "So, who is going to make a gourmet coffee run, along with some seriously carb-filled treats to go with it?"

"I swear you have the appetite of a thirteen-year-old boy. Although, I do kind of like the sound of that. Not the thirteen-year-old boy part ... the ... you know what I mean." De Silva said while laughing her way into her office with the rest of them.

"There's something for you to do, Justin," Hewitt suggested while taking off his coat and hanging it on the coat rack behind the office door.

"What? Be an errand boy for you guys? C'mon!"

"Just this once. Give us a few minutes to set up shop here, and it'll get you out of here for a bit."

Having said that, Hewitt looked over at De Silva as she gave a sideways smirk while tilting her head, as she tossed the keys over to Justin. "No side trips anywhere. There's a little coffee shop approximately a mile east of here. Hang a left as you exit the parking lot. You can't miss it. I don't remember what it is called. Something like 'Mistah Barista.' Sort of a play on words for the whole 'Mr. Coffee' thing."

"Well, that's pretty clever. Guess I can't miss it then. Am I just getting your basic coffee?"

"Oh! Get me one of those, no two, of those cannoli's. They have the best in town. Hard to find a good cannoli in Florida. Hard to find any good authentic

Italian pastries anywhere in Florida." Ortega was practically salivating with just the mere mention of it all.

Hewitt walked over to Justin and handed him $50. "Just get whatever looks good, and four coffees. I'm sure everything there will be pricey. If you get lost somehow, just give me a call."

"That'd be pretty lame if I get lost within a mile of here. Didn't need this much money for coffee and donuts fifteen years ago, that's for sure," he said as he stuffed the money in the front pocket of his jeans. "I guess I'll be right back."

Justin made his way back down the hall towards the main entrance, after stopping and talking to the desk sergeant to advise them that he'd be back shortly after his coffee run.

As he walked over to the car, he tried to keep his eyes looking straight ahead. Doing what he could to avoid looking around too much for fear of what he might see. Although he didn't expect to see too much in and around the police station, he somehow felt he would see more than he was prepared to see once he drove away from it.

He had been driving for a while before realizing he had to have driven more than a mile. No doubt he had passed the fancy coffee shop a few minutes ago, and several blocks back. Given the fact he surely drove past it, he wasn't too bad off since he'd only been driving in a straight line. All he had to do was make a U-turn and drive back. As he headed to the next signal light, he noticed a group of people sitting outside at a local eatery on the corner to his left. While that wasn't so much what caught his attention, it was one of the people seated outside. A young man wearing a white tank top, shorts, and flip-flops. He was seated with a small group of men. It looked like they were just having drinks, enjoying the weather outside. Not too cool, not too warm. Quite pleasant actually. What primarily caught his attention though, was the man in the tank top.

In the moments he had while waiting for his green arrow, he saw exactly what he knew he would. That light, faint glow coming from the left shoulder of one of the men sitting at that table. His new life, the sight of his new life. His new normal. Something he now had to accept no matter where he went from here on out. He will undoubtedly see it no matter where he was, no matter who he was with, no matter what he was doing outside of his home at night. Or so he thought only at night. Earlier in the daylight proved that theory wrong. So long as it was out in public, this would be his life from here on out.

He could either isolate himself, and cut himself off from the world outside, or he could use it to benefit others looking for justice in the same manner that he was looking for it. In that moment, he made up his mind while waiting at the light. In what seemed like hours while he traveled to the various thoughts in his head, was truly only at the most two minutes. He was only brought back to where he was at that light when the car behind him began honking. He shook his head, blinked his eyes, and waved his right hand up in the air to indicate he was sorry for not having been paying closer attention.

As he was making his U-turn, he glanced at the man that caught his attention. They locked eyes for just a few seconds. Justin realized in those seconds that he had just looked into the eyes of a killer. Though he didn't have a chance to get the name of the victim, he now had his first real encounter out of the way. He got through that first case of nerves.

In a sense, he was glad he had missed the coffee shop. Maybe he was supposed to have driven past it, just so he would have the time to deal with his first solo experience, in order to understand how he would be able to deal with what lie ahead. He felt bad for the victim's name that he didn't get to see, but eventually that man would meet his maker, without his help.

Just up ahead he saw the coffee shop. He put his right blinker on and pulled into the parking lot. Parking right in front of the main entrance, he turned off the car and headed inside. Once inside, he was overwhelmed with all the different choices. A sudden feeling that all eyes were on him, unnerved him. As if he were some alien from another planet. Trying not to seem too out of his element, uncomfortable, or nervous, he stuck with what seemed to be the most basic of coffees that were suggested to him. He then ordered the pastries, paid for everything and headed back to the police station.

Though the detectives insisted that he just go back to the hotel, he didn't want to waste any time jump-starting the reason he was there. He knew it would be a long night, so he even bought himself coffee and a couple pastries. He was ready, willing, and able to do whatever was necessary to connect those dots that would lead to his mom's killer. If it started with a sleepless night, then so be it. He was not only about to begin the journey that he knew in his heart of hearts he was meant to continue for the rest of his life, but he's also about to discover a whole new appreciation for caffeine, detective style. Not exactly the all-nighter he had in mind, but if they could do it, so could he.

As he walked into the main lobby, he checked in with the front desk sergeant again, and headed back to Detective De Silva's office.

Ortega was, of course, first to greet him.

"Ah, the refueling elements I have been waiting for," she said as she grabbed one of the hot cups of coffee and a pastry. "You must have taken the scenic route back."

"Yeah, got a bit distracted due to … "

"Hold on Ortega! That wasn't the pastry you asked for."

"Cool your little jets there, De Silva. Justin seems to have brought in plenty to go around."

"Well, then you should have asked for more than the one you wanted, instead of what you now have between your grubby paws."

"Can I just say that I think we need to be more concerned with getting our timeline on the board here, instead of complaining about who gets which pastry?" Hewitt suggested as he pinned 3" x 5" cards with the names of everyone linked to their investigation along the top of a giant corkboard.

De Silva and Ortega stared at each other for a few seconds, before looking back at the corkboard.

"Okay." De Silva stood in front of and stared at the board with her right arm wrapped around her waist, while tapping her left fingers on her chin. Ortega took a seat on the edge of a table that had some files, and a few piles of paper on it. Chewing on a very big danish in one hand, and sipping on coffee held in the other. She watched intently while Hewitt continued to pin cards.

"I saw a murderer," Justin blurted out, catching them all completely off guard.

They all stopped and almost in sync, turned their heads to face him.

"You what? Why didn't you..." Hewitt says before Justin interrupts him.

"That's what distracted me. That's what made it a scenic route back here. Before you say why didn't I call, I didn't have a chance to do anything." Justin walks over to the window behind De Silva's desk and peeks between the blinds. "I was at a stoplight. I had accidentally driven past the coffee shop, and saw this guy sitting with some other people outside of this little sidewalk café place. He was wearing a tank top and I saw the glow from a name on his shoulder. I couldn't make out the name completely because I had a green arrow and had to make a U-turn. But we kinda locked eyes with each other as I was making the turn. It was pretty weird. It was pretty much the first time for me since my release. Well, other than that guy we saw earlier. But the first time for me while I've been alone." He removes his hand from between the blinds and goes to sit down in a chair next to the table that Ortega is sitting on.

Ortega stands up and faces him. "You okay?"

"Yeah. I'm cool. I mean. I came to Detective Hewitt, now you and Detective De Silva, knowing this is what my life is now. Seeing what I see. Knowing that because of what I see, I have the power to change and potentially ruin someone's life. In the very brief moment that he and I locked eyes, it was if he knew that I knew what he'd done, you know? That's crazy, I know. I mean, I know he couldn't know. It was just such a strange feeling. This is my life now. I have no choice. Whatever it is that has me seeing those names, there is nothing I can do to change that. It took for me to see that first hand, by myself, to realize and really, truly accept that, you know?

"And I know the whole thing must be hard to swallow for all of you. Especially you and Detective De Silva. Probably for you too, Hewitt. Until I can prove myself, I'm sure you are all just going through the motions here, but I do want to thank you ahead of time for helping me out. I just want to do whatever needs to be done to find whoever killed my mom. Seeing what I saw tonight has just given me the extra little motivation I need to really ignite that fire in me to get this off the ground."

De Silva grabbed a chair and placed it next to Justin, so he could take a seat.

"Listen, the detective in me wants to go and see what we can, to follow up on the man you saw tonight. Find out who he was, and those with him. But I don't want to take the focus off what we've started here. Like earlier, we don't want to start on a wild goose chase into some new investigation. I've known Detective Hewitt a long time. We've worked on a couple strange cases together, while working your mom's case as well. I know you feel like you really have to prove yourself, not only in your mind, but to us. I can't begin to know what it's like to be in your shoes. To have been in prison during the time of a terrible loss in your family. To see what you see. The feeling of remorse for the victims belonging to the names you see. I just want you to know, that if Detective Hewitt has the belief and the faith enough to bring you all the way out here, then we share in that as well. We may be going on some blind faith here, but my gut, and I'm sure I speak for Detective Ortega too, is telling me you're not wasting our time and leading us on a wild goose chase of your own. That being said, are you ready to light this bonfire of an investigation up?"

Justin looked over at Detectives Hewitt and Ortega, before looking back at De Silva. Grabbing his coffee and taking a big swig of it, he responded by saying, "I'll get the lighter fluid."

Chapter 24

"Hey Dad, how you doing?" Justin said to his dad David the next morning in an early call he made while having some coffee in his hotel room.

"Justin! Good to hear from you, son. I'm doing well, thanks. How you holding up?"

"I'm doing okay. I'm sorry I haven't been in touch as much as I'd like to, let alone having spent much time with each other, when I *have* been home. Lots going on out here."

"That's okay. I know how important it is for you to be out there. Have they made you an honorary detective yet?" David said with a chuckle.

Justin smiling at hearing his dad laugh a little. "No, not yet. I'm just doing all I can to help them gather up more information that might lead to mom's killer. So far, it's been going well. There are some promising leads. There'll be some people that we are going to try and talk to today. Hopefully that doesn't take us to a dead end. I'll keep you posted."

"That sounds good. Thanks for doing all that you're doing there, son. Your mom would be so proud of you. I'm proud of you. You already know we forgive you for what you did. Looks like this might be the silver lining for you."

"Maybe. Time will tell, I guess."

There was a long pause. Justin had still not fully explained all that he was. Not feeling confident about how his father may react. So now, his own anxiety keeps him from really divulging all the details of just exactly how he is helping out with the detectives. He's sure that his dad would be very confused, puzzled, and unsure of how something like that could be. Then again, so was Justin.

He stared out of his hotel window, hearing his dad tell him about his latest project: working on a friend's motorcycle, pretty much from the ground up, so to speak. Justin can picture him standing in the garage, surrounded by his multitude of tools and tool chests, parts strewn all over various shelves, counters, and on the floor. Garage door open to let in some of that fresh sunlight and air.

Garages held a bittersweet memory in Justin's mind. For it was a garage where he began his road to prison. Hard to imagine that it was more than fifteen years ago. So much had happened, so much had changed. Not only had the world changed around him, but he'd changed too. He finally admitted to himself that he'd grown up, and he alone was responsible for all his actions. He could no longer be as selfish as he was before going to prison, thinking that there would be no consequences to his actions, wrong or right. His parents truly did do the best they could. All of this went through his head while his dad continued to talk.

"That sounds great, Dad. Guess you have your hands full there, keeping busy. I'll get back as soon as I can. But not unless I'm happy that the detectives here have a clear path to those responsible. I know you did all you could to be strong not only for yourself, but to be supportive of me while I was away. I just want you to know again how very appreciative I am for your support before and after my release. I am going to do all I can to help them find the bastards responsible. I give you my word."

"I know you're appreciative, Justin. I do. You're my son first and foremost. No matter what you do. No matter what anyone says. I love you. Your mom loved you, and I know she is up there watching over you and guiding you in everything you do. She'll always be there even if you can't see her. I'm sure that if she could, she would tell you who it was. She's the only one who can right now. Please tell the detectives I appreciate them letting you lend a hand wherever you can. Guess they're confident you have something to help them with, having been in the system for so long. Giving them an insider's look, I guess. They must have more faith in you than I give them credit for."

"Heh, I guess they do. I'm sure if Mom could tell me, she'd say she has faith too." It was in that moment, when he said that to his dad, that it occurred to him. She was telling him. She was guiding him. With some form of witchcraft, or supernatural, paranormal, whatever…

that had to be the connection. Her. He knew it was some form of *not of this world,* something or other. But he couldn't figure out who, or what would have triggered it. And the why. It was her. She was spelling it out for him. Maybe she couldn't show him the actual name of the killer, because that person was still alive. So, the only way she could show him would be through the various connected victims that would lead him to her killer. He and the detectives had played with the idea of some supernatural explanation for it all. He didn't even remotely imagine it could be his own mom lighting the way for him, especially in this manner.

"Hey Dad, I'm going to go for now. But I will keep you posted on things over here, okay? It was really good to talk to you. Take care of yourself. I'll give you a call later this week. I love you, Dad. Thanks for everything."

"Sure, son. No problem. You take care of yourself. I can't wait until we can spend some catch-up time together. I love you, too. Talk to you soon."

With that, Justin ended the call and went to knock on the door connecting his and Detective Hewitt's room. Right as he was about to knock, his cell phone rang. It was De Silva.

"Justin. I'm glad I caught you. I'm also glad you initially drove past the coffee shop last night."

"Why? What happened?"

"Look, I know I told you that we really needed to just focus on your mom's case right now. Well, in a sense, we still are."

"Can you hit the fast-forward button for me, Detective? Not sure what you're talking about."

"Okay. So, I've been up all night. I really did pull an all-nighter. On a whim, I reached out to one of my judge pals, and called in a favor so to speak. It's all on the up and up, no worries. I asked her to grant me a warrant for the security cameras for that outdoor café you passed. The one where you saw that guy with the name you couldn't make out? Well, took a few hours but I got the recordings. He was sporting a tattoo that is typically linked to one of our known gangs out here. I called one of my buddies with our gang unit, and he recognized the guy. I ran the name of the guy, and it turns out he is the son of one of the names on our little list here."

"Really? Holy shit! Sorry."

"Ha! You kidding? I've heard worse, I'm in law enforcement after all, but I do appreciate the chivalry."

"Did you already tell Ortega and Hewitt? I was just about to knock on the door to his room."

"Yes, I conferenced them a while ago. They know. I told Hewitt to get the two of you down here to the station as soon as he's able to. I don't want to miss this slight window of opportunity here. If you say he was staring at you with any degree of concern, I don't want the guy to feel spooked for any reason and take off. Right now, he is our foot in the door of this investigation. Don't know what took your mind off where you were going, but whatever it was, I'm glad.

Someone is watching over you and feeding you the tidbits of information that we need."

"Yeah, I'm pretty sure I know who the tidbits of information are being left by. Hewitt is knocking on my door now, so I guess we'll see you soon." Ending the call, he opened the door for Hewitt. "Just got off the phone with De Silva, and it sounds like we're headed to the station sooner, rather than later."

"Yup. You ready?"

"Yeah, oddly enough I was just about to knock on your door when she called. Seems things are sort of falling into place here, without even trying."

"Don't get too confident. Because the minute you do, that's when things start to fall out of place."

"No, I'm not. I just have a good feeling about this."

"Good, let's take you and that good feeling and head on out of here. We want to jump on this as soon as we can."

"So I hear. Let's go. We have some bad guys to round up," Justin said as he was closing his connecting hotel room door behind him. He then followed Hewitt out of his hotel room door.

"Don't forget. You still have to let us do the actual police work. Okay?" Hewitt then shut his hotel room behind them both.

"I will, I promise." He then pressed the elevator button that would take them both down to the main lobby. "You know it's all kind of crazy how things happen. A person can go nuts thinking about how things come to be. How people end up in your life. Why certain people end up in your life. Hell, even why people do the things they do. You know? I mean. Take me, for example. I was just your average teenage kid. Raised in your average middle-class suburban home. Two hard-working parents. I wasn't spoiled. I was raised to appreciate what I had. To earn what I wanted, by studying hard, applying myself, and helping those that couldn't help themselves."

The elevator opened to the main lobby. They made their way outside through the parking lot, over to the rental car that Hewitt had secured to get them around town when not with the other detectives. He pressed the key fob and unlocked both their doors. Once inside the car, Hewitt picked up and continued their conversation.

"A lot has happened since your release. I know it must seem like your life is now stuck in a somewhat of a fast-forward mode."

"Well, and it's not even so much that. I mean, it's like, so many different things, or events must happen for perhaps, just one significant or otherwise insignificant, thing to take place. Makes a person constantly wonder why. Like maybe I was meant to go to prison for my crimes, because somehow, somewhere, in some strange supernatural time travel, or time warp kind of thing, I needed to—to be here in this moment, in this car with you, tracking down my mom's killer." He looked over at Hewitt to see his reaction. All Hewitt did was cock his head to one side as if to say 'maybe.' "I will say this much. I am fairly certain that my mother is the reason I am seeing what I am seeing."

"Why? What makes you say that?"

"I don't know. I think maybe it was a conversation that I had with my dad earlier that somewhat convinced me of it. Not that he knew it. Just by him saying how my mom continues to watch out for me, something as simple as that. I mean you yourself said that she dabbled in that black magic, or witchcraft stuff. What if because of her dabbling in it, that's what is giving me the ability to see the victims' names?"

"I suppose that could be. Never thought of that. But at this point, I guess anything is possible."

"Well, whatever the reason, as weird and surreal as it may be, I'm glad that it somehow is proving it's worth right now. Wasn't sure how soon I might be able to prove to you all that I'm not some whacko."

Chapter 25

Hewitt and Justin sat down across from De Silva's desk, while Ortega popped open her choice for caffeine. Something that had more sugar in it than ten candy bars combined. She would most certainly be bouncing off the walls for the rest of day.

"Okay, so here's what I found. I told you how I came to find out about the guy you saw at the outdoor café. Well, his name is Francisco Massucci. He's the son of Damon Massucci. Massucci is a well-known name amongst the Mafia elite. Now, Damon has been keeping himself somewhat secluded, and hasn't surfaced too much but for a few vacation trips with the family here and there. While the Mafia still has its tentacles out in a variety of different places, we've maintained a low-profile eye on as much as we can. Mostly small-time stuff. Things that slowly chip away at their little empire. If this is something that will give us what we need to really put the hammer to that empire, then we will come at him with all we have." De Silva stared at Justin with an excitement in her eye that Ortega only saw when she knew they were on to something big.

"We know you weren't able to see the name well enough when you saw Francisco, Justin, so what we're going to do is we're going to ask nicely for him to come in, so we can ask him a few questions about a robbery in the area. We can definitely spin it that we're questioning everyone that the surveillance cameras picked up nearby. We can have you watching in the room next door, so you can get a good look at the name you see. That way you don't have to worry about him seeing you up close and personal." Ortega then looked at Hewitt after explaining their plan to Justin. Justin sat quietly with both hands rubbing his knees indicating he was a bit nervous about it all.

Hewitt turned towards Justin. "I know this is the first time you've experienced this to this degree. Let alone outside of prison walls. Also, not to mention, working alongside homicide detectives. That works both ways, you know. This is the first time we've experienced working alongside someone who can see what you see. So, if it makes you feel any better, we're just as nervous. He won't see you. I'm sure you already knew that. And this all sounds really solid. Sometimes you have to go with your gut on things. Fantastic work."

"It's not even so much as to whether he'll see me or not. I just don't want to waste anyone's time. I mean, I want to catch her killer so bad that if this really does get us somewhere, I don't want to feed into that mentality of what got me in prison in the first place. You know what I mean?"

"We do." Justin turned and looked at De Silva again, once she said that. She walked around her desk and sat on the corner closest to where he was sitting. "It's not a waste of time. Time is only wasted if you regret not taking it. I'm fairly certain I speak for Detectives Ortega and Hewitt when I say we work with no regrets."

"Thanks, Detective. Well, Detectives." They all shared a few glances at each other.

Detective De Silva got up, and walked back behind her desk and sat down again, while Ortega went over to fix herself another cup of coffee that she truly didn't need.

Chapter 26

"So, here is what's next. Detective Ortega and I will go pickup Francisco. I want you and Detective Hewitt to wait here. I will come and get you when we get back." With that she nodded at Ortega, and the two women promptly got up and headed out of the office.

Justin stood up and put both hands in his front pockets. He walked over behind the desk to look out the window. Hewitt could clearly see how his nerves were starting to get the better of him. As Justin started to pace, Hewitt got up and made himself a cup of tea. "Maybe you should have a cup with me. Might help you relax a little before they come back."

"No thanks."

"I know it's a little nerve-racking, but we'll be here with you to figure this all out and get to the bottom of it all. This is a good thing. It's a big step in the right direction. Once we get Francisco in here and he gives us the answers we're hoping he gives us, then it'll get easier." Justin continued to pace. "Okay, if there were a rug below your feet, you'd have worn it out by now."

"I know. I know. It's the anxiety, you know? I honestly don't know if I've had this much anxiety even when I was on trial."

"It's because this hits very close to home. I get it."

"When this guy gets here, he won't see me, right? I look at the name on him, and he gets asked questions about some bogus robbery?"

"Not a bogus robbery. It's a legit robbery. Once we get him talking about that, we can then question him about your mom's murder."

"How you going to tie her murder to the reason he's being questioned about that robbery?"

"Well, we will remind him that we know about his affiliation with the gang that our gang unit recognized him from, and that we know who his dad is. No doubt his dad doesn't know about his gang affiliation because that would not bode well for the Mafia ties his dad has. See, gangs and Mafia don't mix well. Bad for business in many ways."

"And you think that he would be more concerned about his relationship with his father than he would his gang brothers, right?"

"Absolutely. He may be a solid member of his gang, and he may have gained a lot of respect from fellow members, but nothing is worse than losing the respect, not to mention relationship and bond that one has with their dad. Especially him. No doubt his dad foots the bill for everything he has and does… well, mostly anyway, I'm sure."

"Yeah, guess so. I knew a couple guys that their own family snitched on them. So, I understand the whole thing between guys like Francisco and their dads.

I didn't have to worry about that with me and my dad. Our relationship has always been a good one. I mean, I know I wasn't the best son, but even with that being the case our love and respect for each other has never wavered. He's always been there for me, as was my mom. Until she wasn't." Justin lowered his head to stare blankly at his feet.

"You're one of the lucky ones. Some of the guys out here, or even back in San Diego for that matter, often don't have that family support. They are all too often ignored and left to their own devices. It's the old story about not enough attention being paid by the mom and/or dad. There's no blueprint. It can happen in all sorts of families. Single parent, two parents, no parents. Gay…"

"Did someone say gay?"

Just then Ortega walked in, with De Silva following right behind. Both Hewitt and Justin turned and faced the two women walking in together.

"Heh, we did. Was just telling Justin here how any parent, gay or straight, can either support or discard their kids," Hewitt said with a small grin.

"Well, that's for sure. Can't fix stupid. No matter who you are, or where you come from. Not that you were talking about someone being stupid. Just thought I'd throw that out there,"

"Thanks for that. So, were you able to speak to, or get Francisco?"

De Silva went and sat behind her desk while typing

something on her desktop keyboard. "Yes, and yes. We went to see if the police unit we sent to pick him up, did indeed do so. They should be leading him into an interrogation room down the hall."

"So how do you want to play this? Good cop, bad cop? I mean, he'd probably smell that a mile away." After saying that, Ortega leaned against the door, crossing her arms and legs.

"Nothing as predictable as that. Justin, go with Detective Hewitt and wait for us on the other side of … let me check … Interrogation Room #7. Hewitt, I'm assuming you know where to go?"

"Yeah. I got it."

"Okay, we'll be there in a few minutes. Just going to grab a few notes here and you'll see when we get in there."

Ortega stepped aside while opening the door for them to walk out.

"Okay, kid. It's showtime." Hewitt then led Justin down the hall, and into *that* room next door to Interrogation Room #7.

Chapter 27

"So, am I under arrest or something? Because if I am, I haven't been read my rights or anything." Francisco said while scowling at both Ortega and De Silva.

Ortega stayed standing, with her usual stance of leaning against the door with crossed arms. Francisco was looking everywhere. Back and forth between the two detectives, and over at what he well knew was a mirror hiding who knew, on the other side. He wiped a few beads of sweat from his forehead with the back of his right hand as he started to get that caged animal feeling. His right leg nervously bounced up and down, his fingers tapping in sequence from right to left on the table. All the tells of a person feeling guilty about something.

De Silva placed a cold can of Pepsi in front of Francisco. "Sorry if you aren't much of a soda drinker, we're trying to go *green* here as much as possible. So, no plastic bottles of water."

He didn't care what beverage they brought him, he needed to take care of his dry mouth as quickly as possible. Pepsi would do just fine for him.

"You're not under arrest. As you were told when you were picked up, we are questioning anybody who was seen on surveillance cameras, where a robbery not far from the *Mistah Barista* coffee shop took place."

"Hey man, I told the officers that picked me up that I don't know nothing about no robbery." He is certain he wasn't involved, but maybe some of his gangster brothers were. That must be why he is sitting where he is sits now, he thinks to himself.

"Well, that's what we'd like to confirm with you."

"So, ask. I know it wasn't me. Whatever you're told by anyone else. What do you want to know?"

Justin watched as Ortega and De Silva asked as many questions as they could get away with. He stared daggers at Francisco, whether he was or wasn't involved with his mom's murder. After a few short moments, there it was. That glow. That low light. It might as well have been a neon sign in the shape of an arrow pointing to the face of whoever it was on. That same beacon, lit up as a sad reminder of the injustice committed. He squinted his eyes to try and get a closer look at his face as well.

"You can step closer to the glass. He won't see you. I'm sure he knows he's being watched. He no doubt has been in many an interrogation room in his young life."

Hewitt watched Justin's reaction as he moved slowly towards the glass. He saw the determination in his face. In his eyes. He could sense how cautious he was being. He was also reminding himself that Justin was once on the other side of the glass when he was being interrogated for the five murders he committed.

So, he knew that Justin knew, what it was like to sit there and answer question after question. The nervousness, the anxiety, the…

"Natalie."

"What?"

"Natalie Lewis. That's the name. March 3rd, 2004."

"You sure? How can you see it?"

"Pretty thin shirt. Pretty bright glow. And yeah, I'm sure."

"Stay here." Hewitt walked out of the door, then went and asked the police officer outside of the room the detectives were in to open the door. Ortega got pushed away as the door opened up to Hewitt poking his head in, then asking, "Detectives, may I have a word with both of you, please?"

"Of course." De Silva stood up and started walking towards the door. "Francisco, don't go anywhere, we'll be right back." She gave a wink, and a smile as she walked towards the door.

"Hey what gives? What's this all about? I have …
"

"Just sit tight. We'll be right back." With that Ortega held the door open for De Silva as she followed right behind and shut the door behind her.

"Please tell me Justin saw something because he's getting itchy in there," Ortega relayed while pointing her thumb in the direction of the room Francisco was sitting in, as if she were hitchhiking.

"Natalie Lewis. March 3rd, 2004," Hewitt said to

them while wrinkling up his forehead with a bit of a concerned look on his face. "Said he's positive that is what he sees. Ring a bell at all to either of you?"

"Not off the top of my head. But then again, could have been a pretty quiet case that is undoubtedly getting chilly by now." De Silva stood with a very pensive look on her face, trying to access any files in her head about other cases she's worked on. They could almost hear the gears turning in her head as she started to pace up and down the hall, now with her right hand on her hip, and her left hand rubbing the back of her neck. "Okay, so since Francisco gave us his info of his own free will, mainly his DNA on that soda can, because he felt he didn't have anything to worry about, here's what I propose. We obviously can't keep him for very long unless we charge him with something. We explain to him that since we are questioning everyone in the area that we're also running DNA so that we can exclude the people we are talking to as potential donors at our crime scene. Ortega, you go see what you can get by checking out the Natalie Lewis case. Hewitt, you sit tight with Justin for a bit. I'll keep Francisco company for a little while longer."

With that, Ortega and Hewitt went different directions, while De Silva was let back into the interrogation room that Francisco was stewing in.

"What the hell, Detective?" Francisco said loudly as she re-entered the room. He had been noticeably pacing just by the way he was standing when she entered.

"Sit down, Francisco." She pulled back the chair she was sitting in, away from the table in between her and him. She clasped her hands together in front of her before saying, "You and I need to talk."

Chapter 28

Four hours passed, and in that time De Silva had taken the soda can, to get a rushed work up on it for DNA. She knew they couldn't hold him much longer than the time he was there, so she decided to bluff information out of him.

"So, Francisco, want to tell me how your DNA ended up at one of our homicide cases?" De Silva knew deep down that Francisco would be the first domino to fall in the very much needed chain reaction.

"Homicide case? What the hell are you talking about? I thought I was here voluntarily? You gonna question me about a murder case now? What the hell? Look, I don't know nothing about no murder case. I may have done a few not so legal things in my life, but nothing that would end up being a murder."

"Relax. Yes, you're here voluntarily, and you're free to leave at any time. But, since you're here, wouldn't you rather clear the air about a few things so we don't have to take things further and make everything that much more complicated? Besides, I know you don't want your family to get upset about anything that we may have to go talk to them about… right?"

He squirmed a bit in his chair, and remained silent for a few minutes. "Listen I don't want my family involved in anything. They're involved enough in their own stuff. Not to mention my dad would flip out."

"Why would he flip out Francisco? Talk to me."

"You first. I'm not going to say anything and get myself into anything deeper than I need to."

"Okay, so talk to me about Natalie Lewis."

"Natalie Lewis? Who the hell is that? Don't know her."

"Hmmm, you sure about that?" De Silva decided to roll the dice, since DNA wasn't back. She would just have to gamble on the fact that maybe he has no clue on whether or not she might be able to pull some strings and get a rush on the DNA. Not to mention, Ortega wasn't back yet with anything else on the Natalie Lewis case. Francisco just sat there with his left hand tapping away on the tabletop, while his right hand rested over his mouth. Staring at the mirrored wall in front of him, De Silva was feeling a little more confident in her decision to push him a bit on it.

"So, maybe her name rings a bell. What of it?"

"How does her name ring a bell, and why? Because I have to tell you, I'm very curious to hear your answer. So, think hard and careful."

After about three minutes, he was still wondering how she knew to ask about Natalie. How could she know? Natalie just happened to be a victim of circumstance. Wrong place, wrong time.

"So, what about Natalie? I have a feeling that no matter what I say to deny my knowing anything about her, you'll find something to say that'll squash it, otherwise you wouldn't have brought her name up to me."

"Wise choice. So, save both of us some time and trouble and talk to me about why she no longer walks this earth, and why."

"Like I said, wrong place, wrong time. I might as well get all this off my chest. Whether or not I have a lawyer here."

"I appreciate that Francisco."

He takes a deep breath before talking. "Me and my boys had rolled up on these other guys that didn't need to be where they were. Over near Fox's Liquor Store on Glass Avenue. We had an exchange of words, next thing you know someone pulls out their piece and starts shooting. She must have gotten caught in the crossfire, and got hit. I saw her go down after I shot my gun in her direction. I didn't know who she was or her name until she was mentioned in the news later on. I guess lucky for us, security cameras didn't catch us. Such a crappy neighborhood, businesses around there couldn't afford cameras."

"Yeah, lucky for you. Guess your luck had an expiration date."

"Guess so, but how the hell did you know about Natalie? There weren't any cameras. And I know you don't have any evidence."

"Let's just say we have our ways. Now, the real question is how bad do you want to avoid anything serious happening to you where the law is concerned? I mean, you don't want your dad knowing what we found out, and we can help with that… but…"

"Ah, there it is. I knew there was an angle to this."

"I wouldn't say an angle, Francisco. I would call it… an opportunity."

"You know what, call it what you want. It's an advantage for you guys, and just something to hang over my head. I may not be college smart, but I'm not stupid either."

"We would never say that. We know you haven't exactly led a stellar life, Francisco. We also know how much your relationship with your father means to you. Undoubtedly more so than that of your fellow gang brothers. So, correct me if I'm wrong."

While she waited for him to respond, her phone buzzed because of a text message from Detective Ortega. Perfect timing.

"I'm going to give you a minute to think about what we just went over. I'll be right back."

She knocked on the door, so that the officer outside of it would let her out.

"Okay, so what did you find out?"

Ortega relayed what she found. "Well, Natalie was apparently a victim of circumstance. Police report, witnesses, all say she just happen to truly be in the wrong place, at the wrong time."

"Okay. Well. That actually coincides with what he just told me. So, we can definitely play up the fact that it's been a few years, and that with the advancement of technology that we now have some evidence that can place him there when she was shot. We'll go with that and see if he won't give us his dad after that."

"Yeah, good luck with that. I'm not getting that warm and fuzzy feeling that he'll do that for us."

"I think he will. Simply because I do get that warm and fuzzy feeling. Time for us to drive in the bus he's about to throw his dad under."

Ortega handed her a file from Natalie's case before following her into the room. From the looks of it, she was probably the bus driver for that bus De Silva was speaking of. She's been a lot of things, but a bus driver. That was a new one. Time to put her acting skills to the test.

Chapter 29

Justin watched, and waited, wishing there was a fast-forward button he could press to just get to the person or persons he needed. De Silva looked to be pretty calm, cool and collected in there with Francisco and Ortega. Good thing he wasn't in there. No amount of patience would help him right now.

"I know you want to just go in there and shake the information out of him. You know as well as I do, that we must do this step by step. You know how it goes. Be patient. The detectives know what they're doing. We're closer than we were a few days ago, right?"

"Yeah, I know. This is obviously all new and strange for me you know? Once we get somewhere with this guy, I'll look for answers to other questions I have about myself and what is happening to me, you know?"

"I know. I can't imagine what you may be thinking about yourself. I'll say this. I surprised myself by how easily I put so much trust in you, and how quickly."

"Yeah, and I appreciate it. If I were you, I would have thought I was just some freak or quack, or someone just trying to waste your time."

"I think I put my trust in you simply because you were recently out of prison. So, I didn't think you'd be yanking my chain, having been on the other side."

"I guess we're even then, because now I'm trusting you guys, too. Trust wasn't exactly handed out while I was locked up."

"Yeah, no doubt." Hewitt continued to watch along with Justin as Ortega and De Silva laid everything out for Francisco. If anyone was going to get someone to roll on another person, it would be De Silva. She could turn on the girly charm and street smarts when she needed to, especially if she knew it'd work in her favor.

After about three hours of back-and-forth conversation, both detectives walked out of the interrogation room, and left Francisco by himself.

As they walked into the room where Justin, and Detective Hewitt were, Ortega had an almost shocked look on her face.

"What happened? Ortega, you look like you just saw the ghost of Elvis Presley or something." Hewitt was just as anxious as Justin now to find out what happened.

"Let me just say that although it was a little over three hours of questions, and back-and-forth zingers, it still seemed almost too easy," De Silva said as she stood with her arms folded around her waist, still holding the folder containing information on Natalie Lewis' case.

"He gave up as much as we need in order to go and have a talk with his dear ol' pop. Told us where he is these days, hidden away a few miles out of town. Told us how he is connected to our dear friends the

Florentellis. I've never questioned someone to the point where he gave up everyone. So fast, it would make everyone's head spin. Well, fast by police standards anyway. It's like De Silva said, it really was almost too damn easy. Either way, I'm just glad he made it easier for us to go and have a chat with pop, who I'm sure will be ecstatic to see us. Especially since he figures that the only people that know where he's at are the people he chooses to let know. Won't this be a pleasant surprise for him?"

"Yeah, well. We do need to move pretty fast on this, either way. I will make some calls, and hold Francisco on what we do have on him with the Natalie Lewis case. We can't let him go just so he can go warn dear ol' dad and spoil our surprise for him. No matter what. So, while I make those calls, and get our ducks in a row for that, Hewitt, you and Justin go with Ortega and wait for me in my office. Shouldn't take me too long to make those calls, get the necessary paperwork, and place some very nice-looking cuffs on our newfound friend Francisco here while showing him the accommodations we have here for guys like him."

"Then what? We all go together to his dad's place? I mean, I'm going too, right? You need me, right? Don't you like need backup or something?" Justin said, sounding very nervous, and anxious. His eyes were twice their normal size. He had the look of a child on Christmas morning, mixed in with a lion eyeing its prey.

"Yes, we do need you, and yes, you're going with

us. But for now, I need you and the detectives to just wait for me. I'll make my calls quick, then we'll go pay daddy Damon a visit."

De Silva went one direction, while Detectives Hewitt, Ortega, and Justin headed the other direction.

So, this was happening. This was really happening. Never in his wildest dreams would he ever have imagined he'd be in the position he is in now. Fresh out of prison. Using some unknown force, or spell, whatever it is, to find his mother's killer… his mother's killer. Words he had truly never thought of saying to himself, let alone thinking of. He was fairly certain that she was playing a role in this somehow. Maybe in her past. Her past life, identity, and world. Detective Hewitt did mention something about her dabbling in some supernatural actions. Her dabbling must be connected in some way, shape or form. Has to be.

There had to be someone that knew it as a way of life for a lot of people here in Miami, to have influenced her. Who knew? Either way, he could think of no other way for this to be happening to him. What must have gone through her mind while she was speaking to whoever it was in order to start this spell, or incantation, or whatever it might be called? The whole thing was so incredibly out of his normal way of thinking. Oh, to have been a fly on the wall during that whole meeting. Watching his mom going through the motions of sitting with this person, whoever it might have been and forecasting enough to know that she would need something in place, in the event of her death. She must have felt something would happen to her. Something that would take her off this planet. And not in a natural way. So, it would only stand to reason that she too, had arranged something unnatural, in the form of something supernatural. Now it was time to see what this was truly all about.

Chapter 30

Such a nice day to be taking a drive out of town. If the reason weren't for the fact that they were soon to be some unwelcomed guests at the home of someone they were certain wouldn't be very happy at all to see them. Justin would love to take one of his dad's motorcycles out for a ride through this part of the country. It was secluded, for sure. Took them about ninety minutes to drive out to it. Not exactly a Fort Knox-styled security entrance. Just a very large block wall that surrounded his entire property. Francisco said that as they drove closer to the gate it would open. A flaw that he said his father knew about, but didn't feel he had enough visitors or intruders to get it fixed. Guess he felt pretty safe and secure, not to mention extremely confident, enough to not do anything about it. No doubt after their visit that would change.

His lawless ways did well for him, though. Driving along the tree-lined entry road towards the front door took them to a roundabout with a massive fountain surrounded by bright tropical flowers in the center. The enormous Spanish-style estate was brick-faced, with ornate 10–12-foot gun-metal-grey iron doors and dozens of windows. Two palm trees bookended the archway that let them look back to the rear of the home, where there was a hangar with a small Cessna waiting, ready for a quick getaway.

Justin's nerves were firing off left and right. If his nerves were firing off the way they were, he could only imagine how the detective's nerves were. Yet again, they were used to this stuff. He wasn't. He just hoped that this drive out here and all that the detectives were doing to help him wouldn't be a waste of time.

"You guys are armed, right? I mean, not that you may need to shoot anyone, but just in case, right?" Justin's nerves had him on the edge of his backseat of the car.

"Of course, we're armed. Don't worry. Hopefully we won't need to use guns at all. But we're ready just in case. You just stay back behind Ortega and myself. Stay next to Hewitt, and just try to remain calm. Remember, we are here just to talk to Damon. If anyone is going to get an itchy trigger finger, no doubt it'll be one of his goons. But I'm hoping it won't come to that," De Silva said while looking at Justin in the rearview mirror.

She parked near the front door, and before she could put the car in park, two very tall, very well dressed, and very angry men came storming towards them.

"Okay... okay... hold on!" Ortega yelled out of her window. "I'm Detective Ortega, this is Detective De Silva, Detective Hewitt, and Mr. Justin Ancin. We're here to speak with Mr. Damon Massucci."

"Mr. Massucci don't appreciate having drop-in visitors," Tall and Angry Man #1 said as he towered over the right side of the car, glaring at Ortega before slowly looking around the inside of the car.

"We would like to speak to him about his son Francisco. I do apologize for the unannounced visit, but felt he wouldn't mind too much if we could just take a few moments of his time to go over a few things about him," De Silva said while keeping her hands on the steering wheel, so as not to make either man be the first to use his undoubtedly well-hidden firearm.

Tall and Angry Man #2 grabbed the door handle of the driver's side of the car, forcing De Silva to get out. "Get out. All of you."

Detective Hewitt and Justin slowly opened their doors, stepped out, and stood beside the car. Justin looked around the large spread, with large men to match. Having been in prison with some of the worst of the worst, he really shouldn't have been intimidated at all. However, since this was all personal for him, it did have him slightly on edge. He could see next to the hangar in the back that there was an open garage with some very nice and very expensive-looking cars parked inside of it. Crime definitely paid for Massucci. Whatever it paid, he clearly used it to continue flying below the radar. Enough so as not to be behind bars right now.

"Obviously, Francisco told you that you could just drive in then, huh? You got ID or something?" Angry

Man #2 said as he sized everyone up.

"He did mention that, yes," De Silva slowly said, while flashing her badge and ID. She then watched as the other two detectives did the same, giving Justin a sideways glance to make sure he didn't show his cards, so to speak.

"Yeah well, you caught a lucky break getting in so easily. We're working on fixing it, so don't expect any future visits here to be just as easy," Angry Man #1 said while looking over the ID's from everyone. "Okay, follow me. I can't say that Mr. Massucci will see you. He likes his privacy, but not surprises."

"Completely understandable. We won't take up a lot of his time," De Silva said as she led the rest of them, walking slowly behind the tree-sized men ahead of her.

It was so incredibly quiet, except for the gravel that crunched beneath their feet as if they were walking on broken glass. Along with the light breeze and birds chirping here and there, Justin would never even have thought this to be the home of someone who could very well have played a role in the death of his mother. To be surrounded by all this peacefulness and beauty was pretty crazy when he thought of the people that it surrounded.

They walked up about six steps to the main doors. The doors opened into a foyer decorated with marble everything. Flooring, pillars, even marble vases. No doubt imported, and no doubt a pretty penny. Just past the foyer, there was a huge spiral staircase directly in the middle of a sitting room that was right in front of them. The staircase appeared to be a clear cylinder of plexiglass. Within the wall of the plexiglass was water running through it, from top to bottom, giving the effect of walking inside of a waterfall. The bottom of the staircase fanned out as it led down to the room they were headed to. He'd never seen anything like that before.

As they walked in further, they were led to the furniture in the sitting room right next to the spiral staircase. Decorative floral-patterned pillows sat perfectly on the sofas. Floor-to-ceiling windows took up an entire wall that gave a clear view out to the massive backyard. The swimming pool looked to be the size of Justin's entire house back in Dulzura. Certainly not that big, but it sure looked like it from where he was standing. Even the fireplace on the opposite wall from where they were directed to sit was huge. To go along with the floor-to-ceiling windows were floor-to-ceiling bookshelves, filled top to bottom with what appeared to be a variety of genres. Did anyone ever really read all the books they displayed? Who had time to even read that many anyway?

Above the ridiculously huge fireplace was a very large framed portrait of what appeared to be a picture-perfect family. Very well dressed, not a hair out of place, like they had jumped out of the pages of a fashion magazine. Francisco looked to be a teenager at the time the portrait was taken. Pictures say a thousand words, so it's said. Who could have possibly interpreted the words in the portrait before them?

Interrupting his thoughts as he and the detectives were taking in their surroundings was none other than Damon Massucci himself, entering from the hallway to the right of where they were all sitting. Walking just a few steps ahead of him was Angry Man #1 from outside. Damon was wearing a floral-patterned silk button-down shirt, tan cargo pants, and tan loafers. Not so intimidating when someone is so casually dressed. Angry Man #1 stopped, and stood next to the steps leading into the sitting room while Damon walked closer to them.

"Detectives. To what do I owe this very unpleasant, unscheduled, and unexpected surprise visit?" Damon said while looking directly at De Silva. Clearly, she had that "it was my idea and I'm in charge" look. "My son knows better than to give *anyone* the impression that they can drop in at any time. Let alone anyone connected with law enforcement."

"We do apologize for the intrusion, but would truly appreciate you spending just a few minutes with us, and answer a few questions that your son has now raised," De Silva said as Damon sat himself in a matching chair next to the fireplace. "I'm sorry, did I mention he was arrested?" If looks could indeed kill, her funeral would be getting planned.

Chapter 31

"You say that to me as though it is a surprise. You see Detective, whatever trouble my son gets himself into is none of my concern, even if I do know about it." Damon said in a very indignant tone. He sat straight up in the chair, and most definitely had that air of "I am in charge no matter who I'm with, or where I'm at" about him. He rested his arms on the arms of the chair, while crossing his legs, placing his right ankle on his left knee.

De Silva watched as a housekeeper walked in carrying a tray with glasses of ice water on it, then set it on a marble coffee table in between where they and Damon, were all sitting. She then handed an iced coffee to Damon before leaving the room.

"Mr. Massucci, first of all, let me again start by saying that we're sorry for the intrusion, as well as the arrest of your son Francisco. We only came here to ask a few questions about a case we're working on. We would have come to you sooner but didn't know where to find you. He's been arrested on a case other than the one we came to discuss with you. Clearly he was very forthcoming with how to find you." De Silva then reached for a glass of water to soak her dry throat. Damon Massucci can still be very intimidating no matter who you are.

Damon Massucci. A formidable force, even in a day and age where the term "The Mob," didn't carry the weight that it used to years ago. And it was years ago that he had made his mark by putting his mark on various mob-type doings. He was smart enough to not get his hands dirty by simply having his hired help do his bidding. Not to mention smart enough to never leave any trail of evidence that might lead back to him. Making sure that any city officials on his payroll, stayed silent about any connection to him.

Justin watched Massucci very closely, but didn't see anything he was hoping to see. He felt so confident that there would be someone that would stand out to him in the only way they could. Massucci had to have more than just the two tree-sized bodyguards working for him here. Keeping his eyes open for anyone new, while De Silva and Ortega asked a few unrelated questions for a moment, he saw groundskeepers outside and housekeepers inside. He could see through a window at the far-right side of the house, straight through to the open garage. It sat somewhat to the rear of the home, but the layout of the house allowed a clear shot from the open doors of what looked to lead to a study or office, allowing a clear view to it. There were a couple of men walking the grounds near it, wearing very casual button-down shirts with tan slacks. Given the warm, humid weather, they didn't have the shirts buttoned, and he could see that they were wearing white "wife-beaters" underneath. A term used to describe undershirts, usually a white tank top, worn by men beginning in 1947. Stemming from a murder case of the wife of a man named James Hartford Jr in Detroit. He had beaten her to death. When newspapers printed photos of him in a stained undershirt, the term *wife beater* was born. A story he had learned about from all the reading he did during his days behind bars.

The men all stood at the opening of the garage, talking to each other, then one of them turned to speak to a third man that he couldn't see because he was further inside of the garage. Now both men were turned towards the inside of the garage and were talking to the man he couldn't see. They took a few steps in as the third man started to come into view. And there it was. His heart felt like it jumped over and through every organ on its way to his throat. Once it got to his throat, his heart then took hold of every breath he was taking and held on to it for what seemed an eternity.

Justin stood up and unconsciously started walking towards the window he was looking out. He had to be sure. He wanted to make sure his eyes weren't playing tricks on him.

"Justin?" De Silva interrupted her conversation with Damon, in order to stop Justin in his tracks.

Justin blinked his eyes, and shook his head, then turned around to see that all eyes were on him.

"Oh... sorry. Didn't mean to uh... interrupt... I...uh..." he stuttered as he slowly returned to his seat.

"I was just...uh... admiring the beautiful cars you have parked in your garage." He slowly tried to regain his composure. "You have a car that I thought only existed in magazines. Most spectacular thing I've seen since I've been out here." He spoke the last sentence while staring directly at Hewitt.

Spectacular indeed. But it wasn't the car that had him mesmerized. It was letters. It was numbers. The combination seemed to be the only thing that could make everything around him completely disappear. Just three little words. The three words that gave more than just meaning to his trip out east: they gave him purpose. He knew without any hesitation that this was just the tip of the iceberg for him. His iceberg. If he didn't know how much his life would change, not to mention the direction it would take after being released from prison, he knew now. This changed absolutely everything.

Now, was that time. Time to really get to the bottom of the entire reason for this trip. All he saw now were those three words. Three words, that together spell the name of the only woman that mattered in his life right now. "Carla. Rose. Florentelli." With the numbers "72313" right below. The day she was taken away from him and his dad at the hands of the third man in the garage. It took everything in him not to jump up and show that man just what happened to men like him in prison. He was prepared to take action, even if it meant going back to prison. He ultimately tapped into whatever it took to keep himself composed.

"Mr. Massucci, would it be all right if Detective Hewitt and I here, go and just take an up-close look at your cars?" He stared coldly and dead straight into Damon's eyes.

Damon stared right back at him, and was impressed that this kid he had just met had the balls to even talk to him like they were friends. Justin didn't turn away at all, nor did he show any sign of intimidation. He definitely had to hand it to him for that.

"Sure kid, go ahead. And Detective," Hewitt then stared right back at him, "I trust you'll see to it that you both don't go and admire more than just the cars. My men don't take kindly to folks wandering around without any reason to be."

"Of course. You have my word," Detective Hewitt said with a smile, as he rose to start walking out with Justin.

With that, Massucci nodded at Angry Man #1 to follow them. He then stopped as he watched the two men ge0t to where there was a gate leading directly to the garage.

As they were walking towards the garage, Justin started to whisper to Hewitt, while pretending to motion with his hands about the cars.

"That third man in there, the one with the sleeveless white t-shirt. He's the one."

"The one what? Do you see a name? Who's name?"

"My mother's. I see her name. On him. He's the one."

"Are you sure?"

"Are you really asking me that? Of course, I'm sure."

They approached the garage, and the three men slowly walked towards them.

"Mr. Massucci don't like people wandering around here. And if he don't, we don't," snarled Man #2.

"Hey fellas... sorry," Hewitt slowly said while raising both hands in the air, showing his palms to the men. "Mr. Massucci said it was all right if we take a closer look at the beautiful collection he has here. My name is Detective Hewitt, and this is Justin. Just wanting to admire it with our own eyes is all."

Justin went to stand next to one of the collectibles that Man #3 was standing next to. "Is this a Talbot Lago Grand Sport?"

"Yeah," replied Angry Man #2, frowning as he spoke. "Sounds like you know your cars pretty well," he said, keeping a very close eye on Justin's hands, as well as those of the detective.

"My dad is somewhat of an enthusiast. His first love is cars, so he is always tinkering with them, before spending his time with motorcycles." Justin slowly walked around the car, while Man #3 kept a close eye on him. "1948 Luxury model. Only twelve of these beauties were ever produced." He stopped next to the passenger side of the car, and without touching it he bent over to peer inside of it. "Absolutely beautiful. Bet you wish you could get behind the wheel of this beauty, huh? Uh… I'm sorry… I didn't greet you properly… my name is Justin… and you are…?" He asked this while extending his right hand, and walking slowly towards Man #3, in an effort to get his name. Man #3 hesitantly walked towards Justin, while slowly extending his hand and staring at the other men who were standing bookend style with Detective Hewitt.

"Vincent."

"Good to meet you, Vincent, I bet you have some stories to tell on behalf of these cars, as well as working for Mr. Massucci.'

"Maybe. None that you or your detective friend here need to hear about though."

Justin slowly turned and started walking back towards Detective Hewitt.

"Well, I have a feeling the other detectives will be talking to Mr. Massucci for quite a while. Would love to hear the stories you have."

"Yeah… well… Justin… you and the detective here have seen the cars up close and personal, and I think maybe it's time you go back and re-join your friends inside now." Vincent said while walking slowly behind Justin. He now joined Man #1 and Man #2 as they stood shoulder to shoulder with each other, crossing their arms over their chests, clearly doing so in a big display of dominance.

"Sure thing, guys," Detective Hewitt said as he eyeballed Justin. He nodded and jerked his head to the left, towards the house, indicating to Justin to start heading back that way.

"No worries, guys," Justin said while working on having the last word before going back into the home. He turned and stared back, directly at Vincent. "Something tells me that Mr. Massucci probably has some of those stories to tell us himself anyway. They've been talking for a while now. So, no doubt we'll be back just in time to hear them." With that he started walking towards the house again. It took one look from Hewitt and sheer will to not jump on Vincent and beat him into the afterlife. His time would come though. He could feel it. He knew it for sure. It is going to take every ounce of patience inside of him to work calmly, and patiently with the detectives, to ensure that they do everything necessary, to get Vincent behind bars. Making sure he pays a price even higher than the cost of all the collector cars in that garage, combined.

Chapter 32

As Justin and Detective Hewitt made their way back to their seats on the sofa, they both picked up on the tension that was filling every nook and cranny of the room. Not to mention the fact that all eyes were on the two of them as they walked in.

"And did you gentlemen like what you saw out there?" asked a very smug Damon Massucci.

"Very much so. Definitely much better up close," Justin replied as he and Hewitt sat down again. He stared directly at De Silva as he was saying the second sentence. "Learned quite a bit just by going to see them." He wanted to make sure De Silva picked up on what he didn't say, by just looking into his eyes. That he had seen something. And if he could convey to her that he had seen what she thinks he had seen, then this visit would most certainly pay off just as he'd hoped it would.

"Mr. Massucci here, was just about to tell us how well he knew the Florentellis," De Silva stated. She then turned, and stared back at Mr. Massucci, and hoped to see a reaction of some sort. He remained very stoic, almost too stoic, if that was possible.

"Yes... well... as I was saying my son Francisco

did know their son Marco pretty well. Marco was a good kid. We were just as sorry to hear about his passing as his family was."

"So, your families were pretty close? Did Marco and your son pretty much grow up together, would you say? And later on, did you get to know Marco's wife Carla pretty well before her disappearance? I'm assuming your families remained close as your son and Marco got older." Ortega chimed in, trying to lay down some groundwork on what they felt they already know.

"They didn't visit much, back where I used to live."

"Before your self-chosen secluded digs that we now sit in, correct?" Ortega maintained her stare without so much as a blink.

Massucci stared daggers into Ortega. "Yes, before I moved out here. Look, Detectives, let's not waste each other's time, huh? It's late in the day, and I'm a busy man. Get to the point, eh?"

"Of course, and I do apologize if we're making you feel like this is a waste of time. I'm sure you understand how detective work is. I assume you do anyway," De Silva said with a slight chuckle. "As we mentioned, Francisco has been arrested, and during questioning of what he was arrested for, he actually raised some questions about Carla's disappearance." She allowed a pause just to let that sink in a bit. Basically, a dramatic pause. She wanted him to know they were going to start following those leads to him, or at least to the steroidal animal that Justin must have seen something on.

She continued on. "Would you say you and Mr. and Mrs. Florentelli were close? I mean, I know how tightknit the Italian community is with one another. So, just trying to get some information here as to…"

"What Detective De Silva is taking her time in saying here is, we're looking into her disappearance again and your family's name came up in conversations that Marco Florentelli had during various trips that he and his driver made a few years ago. Any idea why he would mention your family name at all in the context that he did?" Ortega felt she needed to rip that Band-Aid off and fast-forward the conversation.

"And what 'context' might that be, Detective?"

"Well, we will get to that. Look, it's no secret that you've led a pretty, shall we say, less than law-abiding life? Now while we can't, or to be honest with you, aren't really interested in pursuing a lot of those less than lawful activities, we are interested in the ones that involve Carla Florentelli's disappearance. And now that your son has the unfortunate misfortune to find himself on that wrong side of the law, and since he unknowingly has helped redirect our investigation into Carla's disappearance, we thought you might help us out. Or better said, help your son out. Because, though I'm sure you can help him with a bottomless amount of financial help where an attorney is concerned, we can still make it easier on him with any cooperation and help you can give us. No doubt those same attorneys that have helped you out over the years are either dead, or have decided to place themselves on the right side of the law. I'm sure they have also reconsidered wasting all those years of law school." Ortega let that settle in a bit before continuing on. Before she did, De Silva decided to take over the conversation.

"Mr. Massucci, I know we're taking up your time here, and we do appreciate it. But it would mean a lot to us, and our investigation into Carla's disappearance if you could come down to our office and maybe help us sort out some details so that we don't take up any more of your day here. Clearly if there is no need for concern about information related to our investigation, then our questions get answered quickly, and we won't bother you again. It'd mean a lot not only to us, but to her son. And being a father, I'm sure you understand wanting to do what you can for a child. Especially for a child who's lost a parent." De Silva gambled on the idea of his not knowing that Carla was Justin's mom before she became Marnie.

"Wait, you mean Carla and Marco had a kid? I didn't know they had any. Teresa and Enzo never mentioned that. That poor kid. A son? I wonder why Marco never said anything either after she disappeared. We visited with him and his parents from time to time after Carla left, and there was no sign of any kid or grandkid around."

"That's because I was born after my mom left Marco," Justin said while he stood up. "We haven't been properly introduced. My name is Justin Ancin.

And Carla was my mom. Even if you didn't have anything to do with her disappearance, let alone murder, it would sure mean a lot to me, and my family, if you would just answer a few of the questions these kind detectives have to ask."

All three detectives stared at Justin with awe. Damon Massucci seemed less intimidating now. Justin could swear he heard the proverbial pin drop.

Chapter 33

"Sorry for your loss, kid. Your mom seemed like a very sweet young woman. I didn't know she was murdered. I just thought she disappeared; you know. Took off. Anyway, I didn't spend too much time around her, except for the few times your dad... I'm sorry... I mean... Marco... brought her around after they were married."

"Thanks. She was. And her name, was Marnie."

"Marnie? I only knew her as Carla. I didn't know she changed her name. I don't know anything about her disappearance, why she left, her murder, nothing. All I know is that Marco loved her like crazy. Talked about her all the time. Moved heaven and earth to make her happy. At least, that's what it sounded like, and seemed like, the few times he brought her with him for a visit."

"Mr. Massucci," Detective Hewitt thought he should say a few words himself so that he didn't give the impression that he was intimidated by Massucci, or any of the tree trunks he uses for body guards.

"What's your name again? Because I want to make sure I get all my names straight here in case I need them for my lawyers."

"Detective Hewitt. And believe me, if you could

just help us shed some light on our investigation regarding her disappearance, and subsequent murder, we'd very much appreciate it."

The detectives all stood up, indicating to Massucci that they were done... for the time being. Justin had remained standing after he had spoken up.

"Mr Massucci, everything okay in here?" Everyone turned to see Vincent standing on the opposite side of the room, clearly bothered by what Justin knew had to be a guilty conscience.

"Yes, Vincent, thank you. You and the boys can close up the garage now. I won't be going anywhere this evening."

"Sure thing, Mr. Massucci. Have a good night." Vincent gave a quick glance at the detectives, but lingered a little longer on Justin. Justin wasn't moved at all by his glare. He could trade glares with the best of them. Prison had taught him that, if nothing else.

"Oh, and Vincent, I want that security gate fixed once and for all, for Christ's sake!! Whoever you called and used before... don't ever use them again for anything. Understood?"

"Sure thing, Mr. Massucci. Understood. Sorry about that. I'll take care of it first thing in the morning." With that he walked backwards out of the room, maybe in order to hide the tail that was now hiding between his legs.

"Sorry about that. Vincent is my main man around here. He's in charge of all my business affairs," he said as he stood up. "I was very good friends with his parents. They were in a very serious car accident one night; his mom died from her injuries, and his dad died two days later. I was in the hospital with his papa when he died. I promised his dad that I would look after him, and he has been with me ever since. So, he is very protective."

"That's very admirable, Mr. Massucci." De Silva looked around at the others before motioning for them to start leaving. "Well, I'm sure it's been a very long day for you, and we really do appreciate you having taken time out of it to speak with us. Even though we did just drop in on you. If you could see your way clear to come and talk to us tomorrow… here's my card. While you're straightening out your son's legal affairs, we'd truly appreciate the chat. We can see ourselves out. Have a good night." De Silva then shook his hand followed by the other detectives, and finally Justin. "Oh, and Mr. Massucci, I wouldn't mention anything to Francisco about our little discussion here. It would be in yours, and his, best interest if you didn't." With that, she turned and led them all towards the front door.

Massucci followed behind them. "I really am sorry about your loss, Justin." Justin stopped and turned towards him. The detectives stopped as well. Massucci then turned away from Justin, to stare at De Silva and say, "I'll be happy to speak with you tomorrow, Detectives. It appears I have to go and deal with my son down there anyway. I have nothing to hide, regardless of what you may or may not know about me and my family." He then turned and walked back into his office, while they were escorted to the door.

Angry Man #1 stood on the top of the stairs just outside of the front doors, and watched while they all got in the car and drove away.

As De Silva drove through the gates, Justin couldn't contain himself any more.

"I know that there is a certain order of things, and I know you have to follow procedure… but I have to tell you right now… it's going to take everything in me to keep from taking matters into my own hands here."

"All right, don't even think about it, Justin." Hewitt had to remind him of where he was just a few short months before.

As they made the long drive back, they started to lay out a game plan. They felt pretty confident that Damon Massucci would keep his word and show up.

"Okay. So, what the hell happened?" Ortega turned sideways so she could face Justin, and Hewitt in the backseat. All De Silva could do was just stare in her rear-view mirror without having to say anything.

Chapter 34

"Vincent," was all Justin felt he needed to say.

"Massucci's right hand man? What about him?" Ortega asked while contorting her body as best she could to look at him.

"Vincent is the guy. I saw my mom's name on him."

"Wait, what? Are you sure? Holy shit! Could we really be that lucky in that our somewhat first name off that list that Rudy gave us, he would be the one name that would set us on the hot track to our killer?" Ortega says with complete shock.

"I'm definitely sure. That's why I wanted to take a closer look at the cars. I wanted to make sure it wasn't wishful thinking. Seeing it up close removed all doubt." Justin said as he looked down at his hands.

"Kinda puts a big hole in Massucci saying he knew nothing, or that he had nothing to do with her disappearance," De Silva spoke from the front seat.

"Unless this Vincent guy acted on his own." That comment drew some silence in the car. Hewitt thought his idea out loud, of the connection. "I mean, what if he and Francisco were approached by Marco, or Mrs. Florentelli, to do whatever was necessary to find

Carla… I mean Marnie… sorry, Justin."

Justin appreciated Hewitt acknowledging his mother's name. He certainly didn't know her by any other. Hewitt understanding and making it a more personal recognition on his part helped to keep that internal fire going. "It's okay. I know she had a former life so it's all right. She's just mom to me no matter which name is used."

Hewitt half smiled back at him and continued thinking out loud. "Okay, so, Marnie finds a way to get out. She disappears. Makes her way to Cali, undetected along the way. Then, Marco wants to find her, wants to find her bad, but doesn't want to involve Damon or his own parents in any way. What if, knowing that if he were to exclude them from his own personal little investigation, the only way to do it is to use a completely different source? So, he turns to his childhood friend Francisco for help, for some ideas."

"So, he talks to Francisco, his childhood buddy. They put their heads together and come up with the idea of talking to Vincent, and pitch to him what they're looking for in the way of help. Could be they figure he could feel somewhat removed because he's not really tied to anyone biologically, so what does he have to really lose?" Ortega picked up by continuing the idea.

"Sounds simple enough. Too bad we can't bring in Marco to question him about it," Hewitt said as they made their way back to the police station.

"Since Marco can't speak to us from the grave,

we're going to have to gently push Damon into getting Vincent to talk to us," De Silva continued.

"And how are you guys supposed to do that?" Justin asked, taking in all their ideas.

"I think we should talk to him and Francisco at the same time. We know he's going to spring him tomorrow. So, I think if we talk to them both, at the same time, we can see the whole dynamic between the two of them, and see if we can work on getting some info starting there. That'll give us a way to work on getting Damon to persuade Francisco into helping, if we need it." De Silva started to think it all out now. "If Damon is on the good side of the law now, he no doubt would want to maintain that by proving to us he wasn't involved. Then we go with the relationship between Francisco and Marco, and follow any leads there."

They drove the last few miles to the station in relative silence.

Justin was off in his own world, coming to his own conclusions about how best to handle Damon, Francisco, and Vincent. Especially Vincent. Though he knew that his version of how he would handle him would just land him back in prison, that didn't stop him from thinking about it.

How did he get here? He was still asking himself that. So much had happened in such a short amount of time, and he still couldn't believe it. Here he was sitting in the back of an unmarked police car, with three detectives, in Miami, having just left the home of a notoriously well-known mobster, who had most definitely broken the law in so many more ways than he had... and gotten away with it, as well as having just crossed paths with his mother's killer... and was trying to figure out how *not* to go back to prison for wishing he could take justice in his own hands, while helping the three detectives he was with to arrest the man he knew for a fact already... for certain... had killed his mom! A person could go insane trying to really sort it out, to make sense, and to understand it all. More so, people could, or would, mistake him as someone who should be in a "rubber room" as they say, in some mental hospital for the criminally insane or something.

He did, however, second-guess himself, simply because he had nobody to compare himself to. How could someone with his ability be anything but insane? Someone that saw names and dates, as glow-in-the-dark tattoos on those who had felt like killing for the possible thrill of it? He'd certainly never heard of such a thing. There was certainly nobody in prison with him like that. That he knew of. He's likely the only person of his kind. Well, the first that he knows of anyway. Who knew? He might have relatives with the same... should he call it a power? A special ability? What the hell to call it? His gift. Now that he thought about it, it was something of a gift, given that it was kind of a gift of finding the person, or person(s), responsible for deeming themselves judge, jury, and executioner all rolled into one. He realized he was one to talk. Wasn't he recently released for having done that himself? Irony had without a doubt found its place in his life now. He didn't see himself as one of "those" types of murderers though. Maybe that was the mindset of every serial killer. That they were never like the other murderers they heard about, or knew of. That they were special. Immune. Excluded from the stereotypical type of killer. Funny thing was, every murderer was exactly like the other. They killed. No matter what. That was the common denominator. They had taken a life. It was all relative and subjective in a way.

Now, the day and drive were winding down, and coming to an end.

De Silva drove into police headquarters parking lot, and parked near the front entrance. They all took their seatbelts off, exited the car, and took a few moments to stretch every limb that, for the past ninety minutes or so, had been in practically the same position. After a few yawns and rubbing of eyelids, they started walking towards the building in front of them.

"So…" Ortega spoke first.

"Yeah, so. Let's all get a decent night's sleep tonight. Tomorrow should prove to be interesting," De Silva said to everyone as she and Ortega started to walk into the main entrance.

"What are you guys going to do now? You going to do anything else because of what happened over at the Massucci residence?" Justin was curious to know.

"We…" De Silva started to say while staring back

at Ortega.

"We… are going to write up some notes, and then… oh… I don't know." Ortega finished De Silva's sentence while shrugging her shoulders and staring at her, "Maybe grab a bite to eat? Maybe hang out a bit afterwards… girl stuff?" Both detectives then stared back at Justin, and Hewitt.

After an uncomfortable, few moments of silence, Justin realized that their dinner plans were meant to be plans with each other, and nobody else.

"Damn, I'm sorry… I-I didn't mean to… well… none of my business… sorry." He stuttered, and stammered with nervousness.

"It's okay. No harm… no foul," Ortega said, with a small giggle afterwards.

"I mean, I knew you were gay, Ortega, but… I'm sorry De Silva… I didn't know you were, too. Let alone dating each other. Sorry."

"Heh," De Silva nervously chuckled, "nothing to be sorry for, it's all good. Not exactly something that is printed out on my business card. We don't carry membership cards for it. And it wasn't exactly anything we let on about, as far as our relationship goes."

"Well, again, I know it's really none of my business anyway. Or anyone else's for that matter, right? Anyway. I was just wondering that if you were going to be spending any more time on what happened today, if you wanted some help with it, is all." He nervously stood there, hands in his pocket, staring down at his shoes.

"Yeah, I think we all need a little bit of a break. At least just for tonight," De Silva said as she saw Hewitt reaching into his front right pants pocket for his keys, in preparation for driving him and Justin back to their hotel.

"Yeah, you're right. That drive was pretty long and tiring. So, Hewitt, you have your chauffeur's hat ready?" Justin turned and said to him.

"Ha! No chauffeur here. I'll take you back to the hotel, but if you want to go anywhere beyond that, you're on your own. Just ask for the keys."

Ortega and De Silva then said their goodbyes and headed off together towards the other cars parked there in the lot.

Justin watched them leave together, as he and Hewitt walked the opposite direction to their car. He then wondered if he would ever find someone that he got to spend time with like that. Snapping himself out of that thought, he reminded himself to deal with one life event at a time.

Chapter 35

Justin and Hewitt arrived back at their hotel. As they start to head off to their rooms, Justin again thought back and realized that he hadn't been with a woman… since high school. He was so young when he was arrested that he never got to revisit that rite of passage for a young man in his late teens. What was her name? How horrible was that? His first time, and he couldn't even remember her name. Just some young gal he knew through other schoolmates. He had met up with her after a Friday night football game. Funny how he had all but forgotten about that night. He did call her a few times after their brief encounter, but she either wouldn't answer, or she wouldn't return his messages. She crossed his mind several times after his arrest. Since she was the only woman, albeit a very young woman, that he'd been with, he often wondered what it would have been like to continue seeing her. Who knows, maybe they could have been like other couples, like high school sweethearts?

He might not remember her name, but he would never forget what she looked like. Long wavy hair. Brunette. Big round brown eyes. Super long eyelashes. Very tall for a girl. She was all legs. Where might she be now? He wouldn't even know where to begin to look for her. She probably wasn't in San Diego any more. Probably married to some jock. Kids, house, white picket fence. Who knows?

"I'll come get you early, so we can get there before Damon Massucci gets there. I think it would be best to kind of go over our strategy with De Silva and Ortega." Detective Hewitt's words snapped Justin back from the past.

"Yeah. Sounds good," he answered.

"Get some rest. I have a feeling we're going to have somewhat of a long day tomorrow. Good night Justin." With that Detective Hewitt went into his room after Justin waved goodnight back at him.

Justin went into his room and collapsed onto his back, right onto the bed, staring up at the ceiling, his mind racing and going over everything that they did today. Seeing his mom's name on that monster otherwise known as Vincent, making that long drive over and back. As tiring as the day was, he was fairly certain he wouldn't fall asleep as quickly as he would like to. So, maybe a quick trip around town as a tourist. He knew he'd see things, people, victims' names he was certain he wouldn't be able to do anything about, but who knew when he would ever be back in Miami again, so why not check it out? After all he was single, still young, and could take care of himself. He sat up, grabbed his hotel keycard, and placed it in his wallet. He turned off the light and headed out of the room.

Walking out of the elevator and into the lobby, he heard music. Very upbeat, enough to get anyone just checking in to almost break out into a dance. Not being used to that energetic of an atmosphere, he continued walking out into the night, and into the streets of Miami.

As he made his way out to the front of the hotel, he was asked if he needed a cab. Preferring to walk, he turned down the bellman.

He started walking down the street towards several little shops. Bright neon lights were everywhere. So symbolic of the city. What would Miami be without a few pink neon signs scattered throughout? Pink lights, and pink flamingos were just about every other step he took. If he never saw another pink flamingo when he went back to San Diego, it would be too soon.

He walked for a couple blocks, staying on the same side of the street that the hotel was on, to make certain he couldn't get lost. He heard loud music up ahead: lots of percussion, bass, and drums. Valet attendants were running at top speed to get the next car parked as quickly as they could. Hard to believe that even though it was a weeknight, this place was moving at high speed as though it were a Friday or Saturday. So far, he hadn't encountered anyone that stood out to him, so why not take in some of the local flavor and check out what was clearly a very popular spot to meet and release any pent-up energy?

He paid his $10 cover, showed his ID, and walked in. Good thing he met the dress code with his casual dress shirt and tan cargo pants. This being his first time in a club, he had absolutely no expectations. The music was so loud he could feel it in his chest with every bass beat. He walked through a small hallway that had walls painted with the depictions of paparazzi, little lights, or strobe lights, flashing to mimic cameras going off. Off to one side of the wall was a red roped off area where people could stand and pose for photos as if they were at a movie premiere. In case anyone wanted to know, what it was like to be hounded by photographers. No doubt that would be a money maker for the club owners, taking pics early before anyone got hammered, only to get them to pay for them later on, after a few drinks.

Most of the lights that he saw inside were from the flashing lights that were moving like searchlights in the sky from the ceiling and from the floors. It was amazing that people could carry on a conversation in here.

He made his way to one of what appeared to be three different bars. Each of them had lights underneath the outer edge in order to light the stools placed in front of them. Two bartenders per bar, one male, one female. Each wore a black tank top proudly displaying the name of the club: CATTAILS with the letter 'S' in the shape of a cat.

He walked up to a small pub-like single table with two bar stools at it, sat down and just took a moment to take in all the sights and sounds. Within a few minutes a cocktail waitress walked up with an empty tray and placed a napkin down in front of him.

"Hey there. What can I get you?" she shouted, making sure he could hear her above the music, and at the same level as the conversations surrounding them.

"Uh, I'll just have a beer."

"Domestic, IPA, on tap?"

"Geez... okay... uh... Corona please. No lime."

"You got it, sweetheart." She gave him a wink and walked away.

Though being in this place was a good distraction for what was going on right now, not only in his head, but in his life, he couldn't help but think about what lay ahead for him. He knew who the person responsible for his mother's death was. He even knew where he no doubt lived, maybe in a guest house or something on Massucci's property, seeing as he was like a son to Massucci. He knew what he looked like. He had pretty much memorized his face. He of all people understood the whole murder thing. But to do it intentionally because someone told you to was something entirely different in his mind. He had no explanation for what he did as a young man, he just knew that he didn't do it because someone had told him to.

As he sat at his little table, he spotted a woman at the bar, by herself, with her back to the crowd. Could she have come alone, or with friends? He couldn't imagine women coming to a club like this alone. Kind of risky in his mind, but who knew? He sure wouldn't know, since he had never been to a club before.

The woman he was watching was also drinking a

beer. From what he could see from the back of her, she was quite beautiful, with long blonde hair down to the middle of her back. As she turned her head periodically to look at the crowd out on the dance floor, he could see she was indeed very attractive: olive skin, sharp features, bright red lipstick, and wearing a red, sleeveless, very well-fitted, A-line styled dress. Definitely someone that would make it hard to look at anyone else. However, even she couldn't keep his eyes from seeing something and someone only he could see.

There he was, walking towards her. He could see her name on him, just like he had earlier in the day. Justin felt his heart race, his blood pressure increase. He felt as though the veins in his head were about to burst wide open as they pulsated at an almost deadly pace. Of all the places that he could be socializing in, what could the odds possibly be that the two of them would be in this place together at the same time?

He watched Vincent make his way slowly towards the blonde with a drink in his hand. As he reached her, he rested his right elbow on the bar and leaned on it while holding his drink in front of him. He could see Vincent introduce himself by extending his hand out to shake hers. Then he kissed the top of her hand as she reaches out to shake his.

Justin wanted so badly to just bum-rush Vincent, tackle him to the ground, then beat him within an inch of his life, then beat him some more. Now he had to decide whether to intervene or not. And if he did, how would he do it and keep his emotions in check?

Chapter 36

He continued watching, knowing that Vincent didn't see him. Vincent was talking away with the woman. It didn't appear she even had a chance to squeeze a word in edgewise. He was dressed in a silk shirt that was unbuttoned down to just above his belly button, clearly displaying at least three different gold chains, and wore dress slacks, with dress shoes to match.

He watched their conversation drag on. She clearly showed no interest in much of what Vincent was saying. She had her head turned towards the dance floor through most of their conversation, turning back to him periodically just to nod yes or no at him. He couldn't catch a clue with a baseball glove and both hands.

Justin continued to drink his beer, and took a few moments before deciding to walk over to them and give the woman a chance to avoid any further discomfort at the hands of someone he knew was a killer.

"Hey there, I'm sorry I took so long. I clearly don't know my way around this club, they don't have their bathrooms marked too well. Did you decide on whether or not I can get you that other drink?" Justin said to her.

Vincent stared in disbelief as he gaped at Justin talking to the beautiful blonde in front of him.

"Uh... yes, I did... and yes, please," she said while trying not to sound too shocked as to the bold but very welcomed interruption.

Justin gave a quick glance to the almost empty bottle of Amstel light in front of her, then motions to the bartender by holding up two fingers. The bartender nodded her head back at him, indicating she'd be right over to them.

"Pretty small world, car boy," Vincent said as he stood straight up and took a long sip of his drink.

"Apparently. And the name is still Justin... not car boy."

"Yeah... right... Justin. All your detective buddies here with you too?"

"No. Thought I'd check out some of the local flavor here on my own. We got what we needed earlier, so just taking some time off to enjoy the sights and sounds of town."

As he finished his sentence, the bartender walked over with their drinks. Justin reached into his front pocket and handed her a $20 bill, telling her to keep the change.

"Got what you needed earlier eh? What exactly is that?"

"Well, that's not exactly information I can share with you. Not my place," Justin replied, then took a long sip of his beer, never taking his eyes off Vincent.

"I see. Well. I'm sure we won't be seeing you around again anyway. So, enjoy your visit during your short stay here," Vincent said as he finished his drink.

"I wouldn't be too sure of that. You never know what life has in store for you." Justin kept his eyes locked onto Vincent in a display of confidence that he was certain Vincent wasn't expecting. "I mean. I'm sure you didn't expect to see me so soon, yet here we are."

"Ha! True that, car boy. I mean... Justin. Well, I don't know what you and your detective buddies need to bother Mr. Massucci about anyway, but whatever it is, you are all wasting your time. He's a real savvy business man, and makes an honest living. All you guys are doing is just chasing your own tails. So, enjoy your exercise doing that." He set his empty glass down on the bar in front of him, and stared at the blonde beauty between them. "When you're done visiting with new kid on the block here, I'll be in touch just in time to show you what a good time really is." With that he kissed her hand again, and slithered away. "See you soon." He winked at her and gave a death stare to Justin.

Justin traded stares with him without blinking. Once he lost sight of him, he looked back at the blonde beauty standing next to him, staring at him with the most confusing look on her face, mixed with a little bit of shock and fright.

"So... Justin... since we apparently already met earlier, I don't know whether to shake your hand and say, 'thank you' for jumping in at the just the right moment, or 'thank you' for the drink and walk away."

"No need to thank me, but you're welcome

nonetheless. He's the only person in the entire club that didn't catch the incredibly obvious clues you were giving him," Justin said before laughing a somewhat nervous laugh.

She laughed along with him. "So, it's Detective Justin?"

"What?"

"Well, he said you had detective buddies, so I just assumed…"

"Oh, that. No. I'm not a detective, but my friends are."

"Ahhh. I see."

They both stood there for a few moments, looking around at the dance floor. Justin was clearly out of his element, and really hoping that his nervousness wasn't showing too much.

He extended his hand in order to shake hers before saying as an icebreaker, "So, my name is Justin. Nice to meet you…"

"Gia," she said while shaking his hand. "Nice to meet you too."

He looked around and saw a table with a RESERVED sign on it, in the shape of a big black cat sitting down. "I'll be right back. Don't go anywhere."

He walked over to the end of the bar, and leaned over to talk to the female bartender, who then pointed him in the direction of a man near the front door wearing an earpiece and a very nicely tailored suit. After a few words were exchanged, he returned with the man in the tailored suit, and he and Gia were escorted over to the table. "Enjoy your evening folks," said the tailored suit man before picking up the RESERVED sign and walking away.

"Wow. Okay. Now you're my hero. These shoes were really starting to kill me." She spoke with the biggest grin he'd seen on a woman in a very long time. Maybe ever.

Chapter 37

"So. Justin. You're not from around here, are you?"

He took a sip of his beer before answering. "No. That obvious, is it?"

"Well, it was either that or this was your first time at this place. You just sounded like a tourist earlier."

"I'm from San Diego."

"Ahh. Another beautiful beach city. What brings you out here? I'm certain I won't be able to guess."

"Uh, well, long story, but mostly just have never been here and my friend brought me along for the trip since he had business out here anyway."

"Your friend the detective. Or, one of, I'm guessing from the sounds of it."

"Yeah. One of." He smiled while staring at, and peeling, the label off the beer bottle in front of him. Not an Amstel Light man, but it worked.

"So, are you like a detective in training or something?"

"Heh. No. Far from that. Just along for the ride."

A cocktail waitress walked up to the table as they were at a lull in their conversation. "You folks okay here? Need a fresh pair of drinks?"

He looked at Gia as she picked up her bottle, as if

to say "cheers", so he asked for two more. The waitress dropped down fresh bar napkins and excused herself to go get their drinks.

"Gia. That's pretty. You're the first woman I've ever met with that name. Beautiful name, for a beautiful lady."

She smiled at his genuine-sounding comment.

"That probably sounded pretty corny, but it's true. You're beautiful."

"Thank you. You're sweet." She now began to peel off the label of her beer bottle in an effort to distract from her blushing cheeks.

"So, what do you do out here, Gia? And did you come here by yourself?"

"I'm a realtor, and no, I came here with some friends. They have clearly found company of their own. I was about to catch a cab home before I was hit on by Mr. Personality."

"Well, I hate to say it but I'm kinda glad he did. Otherwise, I wouldn't have the pleasure of sitting here with you right now."

"Hmm. Now who's the smooth talker?" They both laughed at her comment, right as the waitress showed up with their drinks. Justin handed her a $20 and told her to keep the change. Good thing his dad fronted him some cash before he left California.

"So, sounds like you and Mr. Personality know each other. Although, didn't sound like a friendly acknowledgment of that."

"Well, I wouldn't say we're good friends. Actually, not friends at all. In fact, if you find yourself here again, I'd steer clear of him."

"That bad, huh? Does he have something to do with you and your detective friends?"

"Something like that. Not anything that you'd want to know about. Just make sure you avoid him if you see him again." He nervously looked around, just to make sure Vincent was indeed not around anymore. Then, turning back to Gia, he smiled and looked down at his beer.

"Hey, listen. I obviously don't know why after having just met me, you would tell me to stay away from someone, but there's something about you that is making me want to trust you. I mean, you're either very trustworthy, or a serial killer," she said while laughing at the same time. Oh, how he wished she hadn't grouped him in with serial killers. "So, don't worry, I'll take your advice." She then smiled back at him, after taking a swig from her beer. "I hope this doesn't sound too forward, but would you like to go talk where it's a little less noisy?"

Justin thought about this for a few minutes. He knew he had a big day tomorrow. But it would be nice to spend time with a beautiful woman. Remarkably so, he wasn't even thinking about sleeping with her. Actually, it would be great just to have a conversation with her. It would be the first time that he'd ever have a conversation with another adult outside of prison, and outside of his mom's murder investigation, with someone else besides his dad, and the other detectives. He hadn't really given himself any time to just be himself outside of prison.

Prison. If their conversation got as involved as she might want it to be, would he tell her? Tell her why he really was out there. Tell her about his… special ability? Or would he just let this entire encounter be a grownup sleepover?

"Well, I walked here, because I'm staying at the hotel a few blocks away. So, I can't exactly drive us anywhere. I can see about a cab for us though. You'd just have to take the lead on where to go, because I don't know my way around here, of course."

She ponders about what he just said, for a few moments. "Hmm. Let's see. Well, there is the obligatory neighborhood café' on the next block over. Drawback to that, is, I actually don't think my feet could get past walking beyond valet here." She says as Justin smiles back. They shared a laugh at the thought of that.

"Well, I can get us a cab back to my hotel. I'm not sure if their café is still open, but if not, I have one of those fancy coffee makers in my room. And don't worry, one of my detective friends has an adjoining room, so you're pretty well protected."

He almost wished he hadn't said that. Feeling as though she might think he was kind of creepy, to the point of her needing protection. What guarantee did she have that he wasn't a creep? Who was to say that he and

Vincent didn't plot this whole scenario? Eyeballing a woman by herself, in a club. Having one of them be the other's wingman. Hopefully she could trust her gut. And hopefully her gut was telling her that he could be trusted.

"Ha! One of those 'fancy' coffee makers, huh?" She laughed at that while staring at him, without so much as a blink. "Where have you been hiding?" He didn't answer, just stayed staring right back at her. "Something about you that I can't quite put my finger on."

"Something good, I hope," he said while spinning his empty bottle counterclockwise. "I mean. I'm not trying to give you some kind of line, I swear."

She continued to stare intently, then slowly looked towards the crowd of people around them. She could barely hear her own thoughts through the loud thumping music surrounding them. Of all the women he could have chosen to spend time with, why her? Why not? She was smart, and he made her feel very attractive. Why should she second guess herself? He did keep her from who knew what with Mr. Personality, a.k.a. Vincent. It was times like these that made her hate being a single woman in Miami. Or quite possibly anywhere, for that matter.

"How we doing here? Can I get you both another round?" their friendly cocktail waitress said, while bursting her big thought bubble.

"We're good. Thanks," Gia decided to answer for

the two of them.

The cocktail waitress nodded her head, grabbed their empty beer bottles, and walked away.

"So, want to go get that cab?" Gia said to him. Justin just stared back with a very pensive look on his face. "I'd love to check out that 'fancy coffeemaker' of yours."

Justin laughed along with her as they both stood up and headed towards valet.

Chapter 38

It was about 8 a.m. when Justin heard the loud knocking at the adjoining door between his, and Detective Hewitt's room.

He ran his hands up and down his face, got up out of bed, and slowly made his way to it.

He opened the door to see Detective Hewitt's face staring right back at him. "Well, that explains the conversation I heard last night," Hewitt said to him, as he walked past Justin, making his way to the coffeemaker.

Justin rubbed the top of his head with his right hand, as he stood with his left hand on his hip. Wearing nothing but a pair of boxers, he slowly walked behind Hewitt after he closed the door.

"What conversation?" he asked Hewitt.

"Ha. Yeah. Well, from the looks of you right now, I guess there wasn't as much talking going on as I thought there was."

"Well, not entirely what you might be thinking right now. Met a new friend, we talked, and watched TV. Pretty much sums it up," Justin said while opening the drapes to allow some light in the room, trying to wake himself up with natural sunlight. Natural sunlight.

A luxury that he now enjoyed, daily, as often as he can.

He had paid for a cab ride to the hotel for he and Gia. They had gone up to his room, had some of that "fancy" coffee, talked a bit, then watched an old movie. When he had noticed that she was getting tired, he did not take advantage of the situation. So, he had given her the choice of either staying, or him getting another cab for her and sending her home. She chose to go home, but not before exchanging phone numbers. He did tell her that he had a lot going on, but didn't tell her what. Nor did he tell her he was just released from prison. He figured that if their paths crossed again, then maybe at that time, he would open up some more to her.

"None of my business. It's okay." Hewitt half smiled while he brewed himself a cup of incredibly hot coffee. He then placed another cup below the drip spout in order to get one made for Justin. "You need to wake up some more. I already called De Silva, and Ortega. They're waiting for us. Massucci is supposed to be there in about two hours, and I'd like to get there well before that, so we can be ready for him. Well, him and Francisco." He then sat down at the small table next to the window.

"Yeah. Of course. Let me grab a quick shower and we'll head down there," Justin said before he picked up his cup of coffee and headed into the bathroom. "Thanks for making me a cup." He patted Hewitt on his back with his left hand with a little too much force, causing Hewitt to practically choke on his own coffee, before going into the bathroom.

They arrived about thirty minutes later at the police station. Parking up front, they made their way through the main entrance, down the hall towards all the other detectives' offices.

Both men walked into De Silva's office and sat themselves down in front of her desk. Justin sat in the chair to the furthest right, facing her desk, bouncing his right leg up and down due to a combination of anxiety and excitement. Hewitt sat closest to the door. After a few minutes, both detectives came walking in, engaged in low chatter, mixed with smiles.

"Gentlemen," De Silva said as she and Ortega entered completely. "Good morning." De Silva was dressed impeccably as always, in a white collared button-down shirt, with a beige-colored jacket over it. Beige-colored pencil-styled skirt, with matching Louboutin heels. Ortega was clearly the Ying to De Silva's Yang, in a white, short-sleeved collared shirt and a tan-colored pair of slacks, to go with a rather casual pair of Bruno Maglis

"Did you two call each other and coordinate your wardrobe?" Hewitt snickered to them as they both got situated in their seats.

Both women exchanged glances with each other, before sitting down. "We didn't have to." Ortega smiled back in response.

"Oh." As he looked back and forth between the two

women, it was Hewitt now embarrassed by his own comment. "Sorry." He had clearly missed all those signals about their relationship.

"No need to apologize," De Silva stated as she turns on her laptop. "So. Did you two have a good night's rest?"

"Well, I did," Detective Hewitt said rather coyly.

Now it was the men who exchanged glances with each other.

"What…? Wait… what happened? Something happened that we need to know about? Something bad?"

"No… nothing like that. Nothing happened. Well, nothing bad anyway." Justin spoke up. He had filled Hewitt in on his short encounter with Vincent, on their ride over. "I ran into Vincent last night."

"Ran into him? Ran into him how? What happened?" De Silva looked and sounded nervous in her question.

"Nothing bad. Honestly. I went for a walk after getting back to the hotel. Went inside a club, some place called Cattails, and he was there. We apparently have the same taste in women."

"What do you mean, you have the same taste in women? Did you talk to him?" Ortega spoke excitedly, almost wishing she had witnessed the encounter.

"Yeah. We talked. It was after I saw this attractive woman at the bar, by herself. I noticed her before he did. Then, all of a sudden, he is standing next to her, before

I could go talk to her. So, I walked up and made like I had been talking to her before he was, like I was coming back from the bathroom, in order to make him leave her alone. Once we started talking, all he kept saying was that we're all wasting our time with Mr. Massucci. That he's a good businessman, and that he's done nothing wrong… blah blah blah. Basically, that he's this model citizen, and for you guys to not waste your time in whatever it is you are focusing on him for."

"Hmm. I'm sure that attractive woman was grateful for the chivalrous move on your part. Either way, I would expect no less from the supposed right-hand man of Massucci's. Defending him no matter what." De Silva took a deep breath, before slowing exhaling. "Okay. Well. I'm glad nothing physical happened. Did you 'see' anyone else? Anyone that we need to know about? Was he alone, or with anyone else?"

"No. I didn't see anybody else. He was by himself. Well, at the bar anyway. Don't know if he showed up at the club, by himself. I didn't 'see' anybody special there either. He was the only one, out of all of Marssucci's men, that I saw a name on when we were at his house. Or should I say castle. Just didn't expect to see my mom's name again so soon."

"Okay. Well. Clearly, we know that Vincent is our guy. And I know you want to rip his face off. I am very glad and proud of the fact that you can keep yourself in check, Justin. I really am. I know it's hard. So, thank you for that. I mean, even if we hadn't known it was him that we were looking for, something tells me his attitude and temper would have eventually given him away. It just would have taken us longer to find him," De Silva said before looking down at her watch. "It's 9:28. Massucci said he would be here around 10 after posting bond for Francisco. So, when he gets here, we're going to ask that they both join us in one of our interview rooms. I don't want either of them to feel like they're being officially interrogated, even though they are to an extent. Ortega will be in there with me. Hewitt, you and Justin can watch, and listen in from next door. There won't be any fun mirrors in it, because we'll be in an interview, not an interrogation room."

"Do you think you can get either of them to give up anything? With Francisco out of jail, we won't have any leverage now where Mr. Massucci is concerned," Hewitt asked.

"Yes, I actually do believe it'll work in our favor. While we may not have the best leverage with him being out, I still think we will have a small remaining portion of it," De Silva said confidently to them all.

"How so?" Justin said, now chiming in.

"Well. We will go along the same line that even Vincent said to you, Justin: that Mr. Massucci may not have done anything wrong... recently. He's been an upstanding citizen, and a good businessman. On the right side of the law... now... but not so much years ago. So, if he really feels he is on the right side of the law, he no doubt will want his new reputation to remain intact, especially if he had nothing to do with your mom's murder. In which case, that would only leave Francisco as our missing link to Vincent."

"So, you saying we're going to put a bit of a squeeze on Damon, remind him of what's at stake? Knowing full well that his reputation means more to him than his son?" Ortega now saw the direction they'd be taking during their little discussion with him.

"Exactly."

"What if you can't get either of them to go in the direction you want? I mean, what if the conversation doesn't work out the way you want it to?" a nervous Justin asked of them all.

"I'm counting on Damon Massucci's narcissistic personality to not let us down," De Silva said in an effort to ease Justin's worried mind.

As soon as they finished their conversation, there was a knock at the door of her office. "Come in," she shouted out to whoever was knocking.

"Sorry to interrupt, Detective De Silva, but there's a Damon and Francisco Massucci to see you."

"Thank you, Officer Jimenez. We'll be right out." The officer nodded her head and walked back out, leaving the door open behind her. She then looked around at everyone in her office, looking to her for a reaffirming look that this would work out the way they wanted it to.

"Justin, you have my word that I... that we," as she pointed back and forth between herself and Detective

Ortega, "will do whatever we can to steer this conversation in the direction that will get us what we need, to get that all important link to your mom's killer... to Vincent."

"I know you will. I appreciate it," Justin responded, then stared down at his folded hands that sat on top of his lap.

"We know you do," De Silva said, then nodded in agreement. "Okay." She then slapped both palms of her hands onto her lap before pushing herself away and standing up from behind her desk. "Ortega, if you can pry yourself away long enough from your favorite pastry there, I would appreciate it if you joined me in the interview room."

"Ha! You got it." Ortega took her last bite, and then a swig of her Red Bull. "I'm all yours," she said as she rubbed her hands together. "Let's do this," she said after one final swig of her drink, before she tossed the empty can in the nearest wastebasket and walked over to stand beside De Silva. Which drew a frown from De Silva. "What? There isn't a recycle bin in here." Ortega said defending her non recycling action.

De Silva let out a sigh before saying, "Hewitt, you remember the way to the rooms, right?" She asked.

"Yes, ma'am," he responds as he shook his head in agreement.

"Good." She then turned towards Justin, "Justin, you'll still be able to see and hear us, okay? There's going to be a couple of small closed-circuit monitors in the spot where the two of you will be. You won't be able to say anything to us, of course."

"Yes, ma'am. I'm good," Justin said, almost unable to contain himself. He had as much excitement as a kid on Christmas morning now, showing everyone just how much he could not wait to get this going.

"Good. Let's do this." De Silva looked back and forth between Justin and Hewitt as they all now stood and made their way towards the office doorway. "Oh... just give us a couple minutes before you guys grab a couple chairs from outside the room and get comfy. That will allow us time to escort them over."

She was first through the doorway, followed by Ortega and Hewitt, with Justin bringing up the rear.

Justin took a deep breath and worked on preparing himself mentally for what was about to happen. Seeing Mr. Massucci and Francisco, knowing full well that one or both of them somehow got Vincent to kill his mother, would bring his blood to such a boil he just hoped he could maintain his composure. There was nothing to keep him from just busting in and beating what he wanted to know out of them. Just some stucco, slabs of wood, and some electrical wiring for safe measure. Well, the protection of Miami's finest as well. What was funny was, were Miami's finest protecting him from the Massuccis, or the Massuccis from him? His target was Vincent, as he was for the detectives as well. Anyone between him and Vincent would just be collateral damage in his mind. Time to get his patience in check and get to the bottom of it all. This rollercoaster ride that he was on right now was really moving now. And right now, the only thing keeping him in his seat were the detectives.

Chapter 39

Detectives De Silva and Ortega walked their visitors into the interview room, and asked them to take a seat. Ortega chose to stand near the door after closing it behind everyone. She crossed her arms across her chest and let De Silva take the lead on the conversation. She pretty much let her take the lead on everything they did together, personally and professionally. De Silva was that type A personality anyway, so if she didn't take the lead, she would do whatever she could to take it.

"Mr. Massucci, Francisco, let me just say we appreciate you agreeing to speak to us," De Silva said to them. Both men just stared without speaking. They both had their hands clasped and resting on top of the table in front of them.

"Detective De Silva, Detective Ortega, I know you appreciate our cooperation, so I do hope that you don't waste my time without a valid reason for this conversation. Though I did say I like to let my son handle his own affairs, I am a man of my word, so I have brought us both here at your request. But you do understand I am a very busy man. Oh, and for the record, I assure you, this will be the one and only time you have me and Francisco together in the same room in this manner."

"Of course. Understood. And yes, we know you're busy. So, let me just get right to it then," she said while placing a tan file folder in front of her, on the table between the three of them. "I'll start with you, Mr. Massucci. I know we spoke briefly with you about the Florentellis. You mentioned that you had a good relationship with them. In your conversations with them, or visits, did you ever get the feel for, more specifically, the nature of the relationship between Marco and Carla? Would you say that from what you observed between Marco and Carla, that they got along relatively well? Did you happen to notice any discontent between them at all… or hear of any discontent or friction between them?"

"In the few times that we were all together, I didn't see anything that was of any concern. Carla was a rather quiet person. She didn't seem to go out of her way to participate in any conversations. I mean, she would respond, and speak up a few times. But I never noticed any moments of her initiating any topics of conversation. She appeared to let Marco speak for the two of them." Damon spoke while looking back and forth between the two detectives.

"How about the way she interacted with her mother-in-law? Since Mr. Florentelli had already passed away." Detective Ortega asked of the two men.

"I didn't see anything out of the ordinary between them either. She would speak only when spoken to, typically. She was respectful." Damon then unbuttoned his sport coat, wrapping his right arm so that it hung over the back of his chair, while leaving his left arm on the table. He glances over at Francisco, then back to the detectives, before continuing on. "She was kind. Polite. I will say this. A mother will never think that any woman is good enough for her son. Especially in our culture."

"So, are you saying that Teresa Florentelli didn't approve of Carla?" De Silva now asked.

"I'm saying that Teresa certainly didn't go out of her way to make Carla feel welcomed. It was quite evident. Not so much in her actions, but more so in her expressions. A picture says a thousand words, right?"

"So, they say. Did she ever say anything to you, anything about her dislike of Carla? Or why she disliked her?" De Silva started to take a few notes on a sheet from inside the folder she had.

"No, she didn't. She kept her contempt for her, for the most part, to herself. She undoubtedly tolerated her simply for the sake of her son. She knew that there were not enough words to convince Marco that Carla would never be good enough."

"Yes, well, sadly, Carla didn't have an opportunity to really prove herself to Teresa."

Nobody said anything, for a few moments, until after De Silva said that. Francisco then started to drum his fingers on the table.

"What about you, Francisco? What was your take

or observation? Did Marco, or his mother, ever show or say anything that stood out to you? Anything that would indicate there was any friction between them at all?" De Silva said to him while Ortega decided to take a seat at the table.

It took him a few moments to speak up. He shifted around in his seat, and then seemed to be putting a lot of thought into what to say next. Clearly showing his cards, to the extent that both detectives knew he was hiding something. Or at the very least, knew something.

"Yeah." He kept his head low while speaking. Staring at his hands, instead of making any eye contact. "Mrs. Florentelli didn't like her." He spoke in a low voice, and sounded as if he had just been scolded for doing something wrong as a child.

"What makes you say that? Did she tell you she didn't like her? And if so, did she say why she didn't like her?" The detectives took turns in asking questions, like watching a tennis match, back and forth. "In case we didn't mention it, Francisco, and in case you couldn't tell, you've raised some questions in Carla Florentelli's disappearance case. So, if you know anything, it truly would be in your best interest to tell us. Especially since your father here went through the trouble to spring you right now."

"And what, get thrown back in jail?" he shouted while jerking his head up to stare daggers at both detectives.

"Is there any reason why we should arrest you

again?" Ortega asked of him.

Damon loudly slapped his left hand down on the table in front of him, much to the shock and surprise of the detectives and to Francisco. "Listen boy, if you know something you better come clean. I don't appreciate busting my ass, and wasting my good time, just to have you tarnish my good name!" His father raised his voice to him, showing he wasn't kidding, and that he meant business.

Both detectives looked at each other, and chose not to intervene, before focusing on what Francisco had to say in response.

"Okay! Okay! Yeah. I know she didn't like her. Mrs. Florentelli, I mean. I know she couldn't stand Carla. She kept complaining to Marco that Carla wasn't good enough, that she didn't deserve him. And how could he love someone so immature and simple minded. Did you know that Marco and Carla got married when she was just barely seventeen years old? Marco told me all about her, her family, her background," he said to both detectives. They didn't want to interrupt him as they felt he was doing most of their work for them. The longer he talked, the more he would divulge, with less prodding from them.

"He said he loved her so much that he didn't care how young she was, or how poor her family was. How he couldn't live without her, and how he wouldn't live without her. But if you're thinking that just because he and I were friends, that I had anything to do with her murder, you're crazy."

Both detectives then exchanged looks with each other, before De Silva stared back at Francisco. "Ahhh. Yeah, see. That last part is what concerns us, Francisco," she said while leaning over for emphasis.

"What part? The part about me calling you crazy?" He smiled back at them.

"No. Not that part," she continued while standing up, placing the palms of her hands on the table, then leaning over, just so she could get within about three inches from Francisco's face. "The part about you mentioning murder, before we could mention it to you."

Chapter 40

"That's the link, right? The link that De Silva was mentioning, right?" Justin spoke excitedly to Hewitt. They were watching the entire conversation outside of the interview room on a small black and white monitor that showed the date and time stamp in the upper right corner. He knew it was all being recorded, so that helped ease his mind... some.

"Yes, I am pretty sure that would be what they call a missing link," Hewitt said back to him. "We still need to make sure that link gets us to Vincent before we do any celebrating. The detectives should be coming out in a minute, now that Francisco opened his mouth and inserted his foot. Something they were hoping for from either him, or his dad."

And as if on cue, the detectives did walk out.

"What happened? I looked away, and started talking to Hewitt." Justin could barely contain himself.

"Well, we told them that we needed to discuss a few things. Give them a few minutes to discuss Francisco's fate," De Silva explained.

"What do you mean a few minutes? Won't that just mess up things? By giving him too much time to think about what he said to you?"

"No, Mr. Massucci knows that any further unlawful antics that Francisco may or may not have involved himself in would not bode well for him, or his precious reputation. So, he knows, and we know, that it would be in his best interest to convince Francisco to come clean. Especially if he feels so strongly about not knowing anything about her murder."

Ortega further explained, "Mr. Massucci has a lot of investors that would leave him so quick it would make everyone's head spin. He no doubt will do whatever it takes to avoid that. And no doubt Francisco won't want to be cut out of daddy's will. Damon Massucci doesn't want to ruin his good name. We get our link to Vincent. It's a win-win for everyone. We're just giving daddy dearest a few minutes to bond with Francisco a little longer before we go back and wrap this up."

The three detectives pulled up a couple chairs next to Justin, and watched closely on the monitors. They all listened for a few minutes as Damon Massucci talked sense into Francisco's head.

The longer they waited, the more hairs that began to rise on the back of Justin's neck. Things were moving so rapidly for him since his release, it was really hard to believe. If things didn't go the way he is hoping they will go, he is going to have to dig deep to be able to keep himself in check. Now that he has embraced that specialty of his, he knows enough about his mom's murder to work on his own if the law can't help him. He would just have to make sure that he stays on the right side of the law. He definitely did not want to return to prison.

"I say they've had enough bonding time. Let's go back in there and strike while the iron is hot, so to speak," De Silva said to Ortega. They both got up and made their way back into the room. As they entered the room, Damon Massucci was pacing. He stopped and faced them. Francisco was sitting stoically, staring blankly down at his hands folded in front of him on the table.

"Detectives. My son here has wisely decided to cooperate fully with you. He will gladly give you any information he has with regards to Carla's disappearance," Damon Massucci said speaking for Francisco. "So, if you don't mind, I'd like to call my attorney."

"That's good to hear. And yes, of course. I think calling your attorney would be a great idea," De Silva sarcastically responded while looking at Damon Massucci first, then at Francisco.

"I didn't do it. Murder her. I didn't do it," Francisco nervously said rather loudly.

"Don't say anything else, Francisco. Detectives, may I step out so that I can call my attorney?" Damon asked.

"Of course. Follow me." Ortega walked him out, while De Silva told Francisco to sit tight as she joined Hewitt and Justin waiting to find out their next move.

After escorting the senior Massucci to a location in the nearby waiting area, Ortega joined the rest of the detectives.

"What's going on?" Justin asked De Silva.

"'Daddy' is calling his lawyer. It appears he talked some sense into Francisco. Once we get what we need from him, we'll pursue Vincent and get him in here. When we get Vincent, we then go after the head of the snake that got him to do what he did." She filled both Hewitt and Justin in. "I am a little surprised that Vincent isn't with him. I assumed that he would be here too. Being his right-hand man and all. Maybe Vincent is feeling a little bit of the heat since he sees us sniffing around. Especially after running into you last night, Justin."

"Yeah, I noticed that too. I just figured he might be waiting in the car or something," Justin replied.

"No. I can only assume he's at home hoping we focus our attention elsewhere."

Damon Massucci walked back over to the room that he and Francisco were being interviewed in. He saw the detectives standing outside waiting for him. He told himself that no matter what, he won't let his flesh and blood ruin what he had worked extra hard at, in order to fly the straight and narrow.

"Detectives. My attorney will be here momentarily. He apparently is already in the building with another client of his. So, his arrival won't take long at all." Both detectives nodded their heads to show that they acknowledged what he said. "I also want you to know that though I may not have led a perfect lifestyle, nor would I have won any father-of-the-year award, I won't let my son shoot himself in the foot. He'll cooperate fully with you. No matter what. I'll see to it personally. You have my word."

"Thank you, Mr. Massucci. We do appreciate that," De Silva said, speaking on behalf of them all. "If you'd like to join your son until he arrives, you're welcomed to do so."

Agreeing to wait in the room with Francisco, De Silva closes the door behind him, knowing full well that they can still hear and see the two men, even if they are alone together.

Justin sat and watched the little black and white monitor closely. He stared intently at Francisco and could almost smell those gears burning, as they turned inside of his head. He felt very bad for Natalie Lewis' family. The name he still saw on Francisco. The name that had started their path to where they all were now. When this was all over, he would make a point of speaking to her family members, not just to give his condolences, but to say thank you. Without ever knowing it, Natalie had played a very large role in finding his mother's murderer. Without her, they wouldn't have found Francisco. Without her, it would most likely have taken much longer to jumpstart the investigation. No doubt, that once they did wrap up with his mom's murder investigation, they will see to it that

Francisco pay for her death.

"So, how much longer before that expensive attorney of his gets here?" Justin asked of Hewitt.

"He should be here any minute. They said he was with someone else, coincidentally."

"Should I take a look at the person he's with, to see whether or not that attorney will win or lose?" Justin asked Hewitt.

"Hmm. Didn't think of that," Hewitt said while rubbing his chin, in a downward motion as if he had a beard to scratch. "I'm sure it would be appreciated in the eyes of the prosecution. Probably best to let them figure it out on their own. Besides we don't want to have anyone else monopolize your time away from your mom's case."

"Yeah, you're right. What am I thinking, right?" Justin half-smiled back. He saw Francisco starting to pace a little in the room he was waiting in. "I know how he feels."

Detective Hewitt looked over at the monitor. "I'm sure you do." Hewitt sat down in the chair next to Justin again, to join in the wait. "Shouldn't be much longer."

Just as Detective Hewitt finished his sentence, he saw a man in a perfectly tailored Italian suit, walking at a fast pace, towards them all.

"Excuse me, I'm here to speak with Mr. Damon Massucci. He asked me to meet him here?" said Italian suit man.

Ortega swiftly walked over to the room that the

Massucci men were in, poked her head in, then asked Massucci to join her in the hall with the others.

"Ahh. Mr. Dennis. Thank you for your promptness. These are Detectives Harrill, Ortega, Hewitt, and this is Mr. Justin Ancin." Damon Massucci introduced everyone to each other.

"Pleasure meeting everyone," he said as he shook everyone's hands. "Mr. Massucci. You said it was a matter of urgency. What can I do for you?"

"It's for my boy, Francisco."

"Mr. Dennis," Detective De Silva spoke up for them, "if you and Mr. Massucci would like to come with me, I'll take you to Francisco."

Everyone but Justin and Hewitt followed Detectives De Silva, and Ortega, to the room two doors down the hallway.

Chapter 41

As they all walked into the room, Francisco sat up straighter in his chair, but kept his hands folded on the table in front of him.

"Francisco, this is my attorney, Mr. Dennis. He's going to be representing you," Damon Massucci said to his son.

"Yeah, about that." Francisco nervously smiled at his father as he now started to rub his hands together, due to his nervousness.

"Francisco, nice to meet you." Mr. Dennis extended his hand to shake Francisco's.

Francisco didn't shake his hand, and instead stood up and faced everyone.

"I don't care about an attorney," he said, bringing a look of shock and disbelief to the face of everyone in the room.

"What the hell do you mean you don't care about an attorney? What are you talking about?" Daddy Damon asked, while trying to contain his growing level of anger, not to mention his slowly dissipating patience.

"Francisco, think before you speak. We haven't mirandized you... or charged you... but... legally I have to remind you of that," De Silva expressed to him.

"I don't care! You guys are going to have me pinned for the Natalie Lewis death anyway. I don't know how, but you will. I just know it!!" Francisco angrily and nervously shouted.

"Francisco, you'll want to think long and hard about this, okay? Whatever you choose to say here, you'll need legal representation either way," Mr. Dennis relayed to him.

"No. I've made up my mind. I'll tell you whatever you need to know. But only if you help me out with the Natalie Lewis death. It was an accident; you have to know that."

Both detectives stared at each other, before looking over at both Massucci men, and the attorney.

"Gentlemen. I need a moment or two, to very quickly speak with Detective Ortega here. Just sit tight." De Silva then motioned to Ortega to join her in the hallway.

As soon as Justin, and Hewitt heard her say that, from still watching the monitors, they immediately went to meet the women in the hallway, too.

"What the hell!" exclaimed Justin.

"Hold on, Justin. Don't get worked up." Hewitt says, while patting him on his shoulder.

"Okay, look. We all know he's good for the Natalie Lewis case. Accidental or not, he's going down for that. He'll want to deal, or at least the attorney will want to advise him to take a deal. That'll be our opportunity to watch him drive the bus that he'll be throwing Vincent under," De Silva explained to them all.

"What makes you think the attorney will want to deal? He doesn't know anything about my mom's case. Or the Natalie Lewis case."

"He'll deal. Once he hears we have eyewitnesses placing Francisco nearby, and security footage near the robbery that he fled from, he'll want to deal. Regardless of what little time, or knowledge he has of either case. Mr. Dennis will know that security footage is not going to be something he can just argue away. All we're going to ask is that Francisco give up Vincent, so that we can all deal," Ortega explained, while looking at her watch.

"Are we keeping you from an otherwise pressing engagement, Detective Ortega?" De Silva asked of her partner.

"Oh... sorry... no." Ortega said, as she stared at the three pairs of eyes that stared back at her in surprise. "I just figured we could let them stew a bit while we got a bite to eat is all," Ortega said with a furrowed brow.

"You mean while *you* got a bite to eat. I swear, it's like having a teenager for a partner." De Silva shook her head at Ortega.

Hewitt and Justin both laughed into their hands, while pretending to cough.

"I realize you have somewhat of a bottomless pit for a stomach. But we need to strike while the iron is hot, you know?"

"Yeah, you're right. Sorry," Ortega said with her head hanging down. "I'm sorry, Justin. I meant no disrespect."

"It's okay. I'm hungry too, but I have a bigger hunger to feed than the one in my stomach." Justin tried to tap back into the real reason they were all there.

The two detectives made their way back into the room holding the three men.

"Gentlemen," De Silva said as she started walking towards Francisco. "Francisco Massucci. You're under arrest for the death of Natalie Lewis. Stand up and place your hands behind your back, please. Detective Ortega?"

"You have the right to remain silent…"

"Wait!" Francisco placed his hands behind his back, but squirmed nonetheless as Detective Ortega started to place handcuffs around his wrists.

"Anything you say can and will be used against you in a court of law…"

"I said wait! Yeah, yeah, yeah… I know my rights. I watch enough cop shows to hear them read all the time. Besides not like I haven't had them read to me before." Francisco complained as he was pushed back down into a chair. That didn't keep Ortega from completing the mirandizing process.

Ortega and De Silva stared at each other, while Mr. Massucci, and Mr. Dennis traded looks as well.

"All right, detectives. Now that you've made things official here, let's talk." Mr. Dennis made himself comfortable next to Francisco.

"Well, before we get to talking, and make like

we're negotiating the price of a used car, Francisco, you ready to help us out here?" De Silva jumped right into it.

Francisco looked around at everyone before responding, "Okay, look. I'm going to just be straight up with you guys. Because I'm not going to take the entire fall for the guys that I was with during the robbery," he said practically jumping out of his skin with anxiety and fright.

"Francisco, as your attorney now... I strongly urge you to..." Attorney Dennis was immediately cut off by a very nervous and scared virtual bus driver, headed straight to an "innocent" bystander by the name of Vincent.

Chapter 42

"No! I've made up my mind." He yelled.

"We're listening." De Silva answered calmly, and as slowly as she could.

"Okay. I'll make it easy. I ain't going down any more than I need to." He let out a big sigh, before continuing on. "Yeah, my boys asked me to join them in that little heist that cost that girl's life. I didn't know I shot her until the news later the next day. I didn't mean to shoot her. It really was an accident."

"We know that. We'll work on that with you and your attorney here. Tell us what you can about the relationship between you and Marco Florentelli. More specifically, his state of mind and how he handled his wife Carla's disappearance." De Silva wanted to make sure she was careful not to show her cards entirely. She didn't want to completely guide him to the information she was looking for.

"I'm not going to lie. He was a wreck. He was lost. She was his whole world, man. He didn't know what to do, or how to live without her. I mean, he was really depressed."

"Was he angry at all? When he first discovered she was gone, did he seem pissed off at all?" Ortega would take her turn at him every few moments.

"Naw. Not at first anyway. I mean, like he was scared. Like maybe she was kidnapped or something. He was more worried, thinking something did happen to her. When she didn't come back home, or call after a few days, then he started to get a little mad."

"He waited on filing her missing person's report. Did he ever specifically tell you why?"

"I asked him that because I could see how messed up he was about her being gone. He said he hesitated, because he figured that he could find her without any help, or interference from the police. Besides, given his family name, he felt that he wouldn't get a fair shake."

Justin couldn't believe what he was seeing or hearing. What an egotistical coward this Marco guy was. He sure didn't sound like a guy that his mom would ever be attracted to. Certainly not someone that would measure up one bit to his dad. He almost felt bad seeing and knowing that Natalie Lewis' killer was wearing a pair of handcuffs, but only as a means to get to his mom's killer. He told himself that once this was all over, and Vincent was behind bars, he would visit Natalie's family and express his condolences, as well as his gratitude.

"What about his family? Were you ever around them during the time of Carla's disappearance?" De Silva continued on, while taking notes the whole while. "Did his mother seem to show any concern, or offer her help in any way?"

"Yeah, she was a little worried at first, too. Then she started to get mad at him because he was so obsessed with finding her. He would tell me that his mom was always yelling at him to move on, and to just get over it. But Marco couldn't do it. He just couldn't shake Carla. You know?"

Both Damon Massucci and Attorney Dennis just stood, arms folded across their chests, and watched Francisco slowly incriminate himself right before their eyes, knowing that there was nothing they could say or do to stop him.

Justin knew it too. He could see that Francisco felt cornered with nowhere to go. He had to know that he was caught no matter what. Justin could only imagine how the detectives must feel. Like leading a lamb to its slaughter. It was an incredibly difficult thing to do, to take all these baby steps when they already knew how it would end.

"Yeah, we know. Did he ever talk to you about using his family connections, shall we say, to take steps in finding her that maybe weren't exactly within the limitations of the law?" De Silva knew she has to fast-forward this entire conversation, but to do it slowly at the same time, so as not to miss a step. That missed step could cost her, since Attorney Dennis was watching and listening so intently.

"No. He didn't. Right up to the day he killed himself, he said he didn't want to do anything illegal because he didn't want any illegal stuff to interfere with his finding her. He honestly couldn't live without her. So, he didn't. Live without her that is. He loved her that much." Francisco just hung his head after that. "I really wish I could have done something. I would have done anything, even if he wouldn't. You know?"

"After he died, did you keep in touch with his mother?" Ortega now sat and started taking notes as well.

Francisco took a deep breath before answering.

"Yeah. I did. Not at first. I didn't call or visit for about two weeks or so after his funeral. But yeah, I called his mom. Just to see how she was doing."

"And, how was she? I know that's a dumb question, of course she was still grieving, but how did she sound otherwise to you?"

"She was sad, depressed, but angry more than anything."

There it was.

"Angry? How so? What makes you say she was angry?"

This was exactly what they were after. They knew quite obviously that Marco couldn't have done anything. They just needed the links that were missing, in the chain they intended to wrap around Vincent.

Justin inched forward in his chair, closer to the monitor. His elbows rested on his lap, while he rested his chin on his clasped hands. It was like he couldn't see or hear anything but what Francisco was saying. He wanted to reach through the monitor and pull the words out of Francisco's mouth faster. All he wanted to hear was Vincent's name. Nothing more, nothing less. Simply nothing else mattered. He wanted so much to just get back to his dad, and start his life.

The detectives knew that they'd be getting Vincent's name soon from Francisco. They were somewhat relieved that Vincent wasn't with Mr. Massucci. On the other hand, it would have helped, too. Vincent would undoubtedly make a run for it, and to do something like that at a police station was legal suicide. In this case, it would be somewhat of an assisted suicide.

Chapter 43

"What did Mrs. Florentelli say, or do, that made you believe she was angry? More so than sad or depressed over Marco's death?" Both detectives were now listening more intently than they were a few minutes ago. They couldn't help but notice the deep breath that Francisco had taken before answering their next few questions.

"She said that if it hadn't been for that opportunistic gold-digging bitch of a wife, her Marco would still be alive. She blamed Carla. She disliked her from the beginning, and Marco knew it. She made no effort to even try and like Carla. I saw it every time Marco would invite me to go with him and Carla, to family functions. It was super obvious too just by looking at her. Well, it was obvious to me anyway."

"Okay. So, she didn't like her. She was angry and blamed Carla for Marco's death. What were your conversations like, while she was angry? Did she ask you anything about Marco? Or were your talks strictly about how she blamed Carla?"

"It was all about how angry she was."

"Did she ever ask you about whether or not, Marco had made any headway in finding her?"

"Yes."

"What did you tell her?"

"I said he tried but didn't have any new information that led him to her."

"What then?"

"She asked me if I knew anyone that would pick up where Marco left off... but would be willing to work on finding her, using any means necessary. Legal or not."

"And did you tell her you knew someone that would do that for her?"

The detectives both felt the hair start to rise on the back of their necks. Even Justin and Hewitt got goosebumps, to go along with Justin's chills.

Francisco fidgeted in his seat. He looked around the room, then took a deep breath and said, "Vincent... I told her that Vincent would do just about anything. No matter what it was."

It was as if Justin spoke Vincent's name at the same time that Francisco did.

"You know... I know you and I don't have the best father and son relationship, but that doesn't mean you have to drag Vincent into this Francisco! Do not make him a casualty in our battle to regain our... whatever it is!" Damon Massucci had just about had enough of what was happening right before his eyes.

"Okay, that's enough. Detectives, it's clear my client here had nothing to do with Ms. Carla Florentelli's disappearance. Now I've let this go on long enough, having allowed you to question him on an unrelated case," Attorney Dennis said, as he attempted to stop the conversation from going any further.

"Mr. Dennis, Mr. Massucci here has made it very clear that he wanted to speak to us without any coercion. Yes, we have arrested him for the Natalie Lewis case, but if he is withholding information related to the Carla Florentelli case, then that puts an entirely different spin on things, wouldn't you agree?" De Silva rolled the dice on Francisco wanting to come clean on everything related to him, just to save his own skin.

Mr. Dennis looked at Damon Massucci, who then looked away from him, leaving it up to him to fight his own legal war of words, basically confirming that the senior Massucci would support his son only so far. Glancing over at Francisco, he could see how he was just aching to get whatever he had to say out of his system, no matter what the cost.

"I don't care about any of the legal mumbo jumbo. I just don't want to be linked to anything other than what y'all are arresting me for is all. So, yeah. I told her that my father's favorite son, even though he wasn't his biological son at all, would do whatever she wanted."

"So, what happened? How did it all come about?" Ortega asked while staring first at Mr. Dennis, then taking a quick glance at daddy dearest, Damon.

"Okay. So, in one of our calls, she had asked for someone to do stuff for her. Saying how she'll always blame Carla for Marco's death, and she wanted Carla to pay for it. Carla had been missing some time, but she would do whatever it took to continue the search, to pick up from where Marco left off. Marco hadn't shared too much info with her, because he knew how much his mom hated her."

"Okay, so is that why she asked you about where he left off, and that's when she jumped on the idea that you knew someone, and that person would do anything, even if it meant that it would be done to some degree, illegally?"

"Yeah. So, when I told her that Vincent would do whatever she needed, it was like her whole attitude changed."

"And did you tell Vincent what she had planned before he agreed to anything?"

"Yeah."

"And he didn't have a problem with whatever she wanted?"

"He didn't care. I don't know if he thought that if he did something as crazy as what she wanted done to find Carla, that it would look good in my dad's eyes. He's always felt like he was my dad's son, as opposed to me. He may call him by his first and last name when he talks to him. But when he isn't, he tells people he's his dad, or refers to him as 'pop'."

"And how do you feel about that?" De Silva now tried to play on Francisco's possible disdain for Vincent, in order to get as much as she could.

"I wasn't surprised. I knew my father favored him anyway."

"Okay, and then what? You talked to Vincent, he agreed to help?"

"Yeah, he was up for whatever she had."

"So, tell me about that conversation with her, did you all agree to meet up? All three of you?"

"Yes. Mrs. Florentelli asked for us to meet up for coffee, or lunch, sometimes dinner, to make things look as casual as possible."

Watching all this unfold on the monitors was almost going in slow motion for Justin and Detective Hewitt.

"You know, it is kind of sickening to me, even though I know I'm not one to talk, but it is kind of sickening to know of, or hear of people just talking about all the bad things they're going to do over a cup of coffee," Justin said while he began to pace.

"I get that this is all a rather surreal situation for you given what you've encountered the past few years, of course. But this is as real as it will get right now. The same thing is happening right now, no doubt, in the same manner with some other people, at this very moment. And we don't even know it. Could be that right now, somebody's death is being planned. Somebody is not only deciding on what to eat or drink at that little get-together, but also deciding someone's fate," Hewitt said while watching Justin walk back and forth, before focusing back on the monitors.

"So, we would meet at different little coffee shops, different little diner places, so that it would mix things up a bit, as far as our meetings would go. But it was always the same conversation. Find Carla. Make her pay for Marco's death."

Chapter 44

What felt like an eternity, was roughly about nine hours. Between waiting for everyone to gather in the room they were in now, and for the information they were looking for, they'd been there a full day already. Everyone was feeling the exhaustion. Their levels of patience were being tested like never before.

With the sun having already set, Justin had wished it was a different kind of workday, as opposed to getting what they needed out of someone with daddy issues.

"All right, to recap what we know so far, based on what you've told us, we know what was being asked of you, and what was being asked of Vincent. We know you'd meet at several different eateries, for your meetings. We know who was leading the charge of this newly formed search party of yours. And we know where this search party ended up at."

Everyone watching and listening was sitting on the edge of their proverbial seats, waiting for that other shoe to finally drop so they could go on with their lives.

"So, we've established that you and Vincent found yourselves in San Diego, California. You both had discovered that Carla had changed her name to Marnie, and that she had remarried, and had a child. You both also knew that her child was in prison for murder, and that it was just her and her husband, with no other children around. You both watched her for days from a distance to establish her daily routines."

"Yes, and every day Vincent would use cash, wired to him from Mrs. Florentelli under an assumed name. He'd use that cash to buy a burner phone that he would call her on to give her an update on things. And when he didn't use a burner phone, he'd use the cash to buy one of those prepaid cards, that he would call her from, under a different name, at a random pay phone."

"You know you'll have to give us that name," Ortega said, after taking a sip from her iced coffee. She had made sure that she was given a chance to get something to drink, even if it was just iced coffee. She had hoped to get food, but would continue being patient if it meant they'd be done soon. Not to mention, she knew if she did wait, she'd get De Silva to buy her a well-deserved dinner.

"Emmitt Taylor. That was the name he used."

"Okay, so once you both had her routine down, what were you both instructed to do?" De Silva was hoping this would be the final proverbial nail in Vincent's coffin.

"Wait about two or three days then take care of her. Basically, get rid of her" He explained.

De Silva would be very curious to then find out how Daddy Damon would feel about all of this. Or if he even had any knowledge of everything that Vincent and his true son had done behind his back, which then led to her next line of questions. "What was the reason that Vincent gave to your father as to why he was gone for so long? I mean, I know you were out doing your own thing, but what was Vincent's excuse? He was living under your father's roof, right? And your father had made it clear to us, from our talk earlier with him, that Vincent is like his right-hand man. How is it that he was able to be gone so long, not being there to deal with your father's affairs that entire time?"

"All he did was tell him he wanted to go down to San Diego for a break, and my dad didn't bother him the whole time he was there. Vincent could do whatever he wanted to. It was never a big deal. My dad always gave him enough money for it, too."

The senior Massucci, though technically he wasn't even supposed to be in the same room at all, was still there, and didn't seem to be all that comfortable with what was being said. Both detectives in there with him didn't care how much he seemed to wish that he was anywhere else; they'd deal with him later. They also weren't all that concerned about any of his somewhat crooked business dealings that right now, in his mind, might be in jeopardy. Right now, they were hot on the trail of his somewhat adopted son, Vincent.

"So, what happened the day that you and Vincent were told to finally put into motion the reason you went to San Diego?"

Francisco took a sip of the soda that had been

brought in for him. All the "singing" he was doing was most certainly drying out his throat. He seemed to be pretty at ease with all that he was laying out for them. This had to have been eating away at him. Not only did he have a father that thought he was a disappointment of a son, but he probably thought that he now had a ringside seat to the fall of 'he can do no wrong' Vincent. He only wished he could be a fly on the wall when they arrest him. There wouldn't be anything that Vincent could do about it either. His father was in here, listening to it all play out. So, no matter what he might say to him, he couldn't deny it. Mainly because daddy Damon had been left out of what he and Vincent were doing behind his back with Mrs. Florentelli. Vincent would then be the newest disappointment in his father's eyes, which would be fine by him. It would take some of the focus off him in that department. He took pleasure in bringing Vincent down. At least he knew that he wouldn't go down for the actual action that took the life of someone he knew; someone he was actually social with. Someone he didn't have any problems with, or felt deserved to have been treated the way she was. Either way, he couldn't deny he had played a role. Just not the role that Vincent had played.

It was all about choices after all. He could have made so many of the correct choices. Choices that no doubt would have led to a more desirable outcome. Choices that would have maybe had him asking the questions right now, instead of answering them.

Choices that would have given him the respect he felt he deserved from his own flesh and blood, but never truly got. So many, many of them. Well, his choice right now was to just be done with it all, and ruin someone else's life besides his own.

More soda. He just couldn't drink enough of it right now. If only he were allowed to smoke.

"Vincent called Mrs. Florentelli that morning. She had told him that that was the day we were going to take care of Carla... I mean Marnie. Still can't get used to the name she had." He continued on.

"That's July 23rd, 2013? A little over two years ago, correct?"

Justin by now had stopped pacing and was sitting down again. Cracking his knuckles, he almost couldn't listen to what would be the details of his mother's final day alive. Both of his legs were now bouncing up and down again. His hands constantly rubbing the tops of his legs. Back and forth, over and over again.

"Yeah. We took a cab to an address about two blocks away from where she worked, and then we started to walk over towards where she worked. We knew what time she got out, so we kind of hung out across the street waiting for her. There was a small park that we just sat at and waited. When it got to about five minutes from her walking out and leaving for the night, we started walking over and as we got closer, she came out."

"Did she walk out alone, or was she with other

coworkers?"

"She was with a couple other women. We went up to her and Vincent greeted her by saying, 'Hi Carla. Marco is dead, and his mom would like to talk to you.' She looked super shocked, and her friends looked at her with a very confused look on their faces."

"Just like that? Marco is dead? Ripped that band aid right off, eh? And what did she say or do after that?" Each detective was taking notes of every syllable Francisco spoke.

"Yeah, Vincent just got right to it. She didn't say anything. At first. After about a minute, she told her friends that Carla was her middle name, and that Marco was a relative. I guess she didn't want her coworkers to worry or question anything. Maybe she didn't want to involve them. She must have known it wasn't good, our being there. You know?"

Justin could only imagine what was going through his mother's head at that moment. She must have known, simply by the presence of the two men, that her past had finally caught up with her.

Chapter 45

Hours now seemed more like days, listening to a total stranger describe the last moments of his mother's life. Like he was watching a movie with him in the lead role. He must be patient a little bit longer. He was slowly trying to convince himself to do that.

He had practically memorized every nook and cranny of every wall he has been pacing in front of. The ever-present bland colors meant to promote a calm and quiet environment. When he got a job, he would make sure that it wasn't in an office with the same colors. Maybe not an office at all. Not to mention the smell of burnt coffee, and stale food mixed with a small serving of nicotine. Very cliché. He wondered if his life would ever not involve law enforcement. Men and women in business attire, uniforms, guns in holsters. Everything one would associate with a police department. Would he ever be free of this type of environment?

His thoughts were interrupted when he and Hewitt saw De Silva and Ortega come out of the interview room and start speaking to the officers outside of it. Ortega walked back into the interview room, and exited with Francisco in handcuffs, handing him off to a uniformed police officer standing there.

The three detectives and Justin all met halfway between where Justin and Detective Hewitt had been watching on the closed-circuit monitors. Justin could hardly contain himself; he was so pumped to get some results.

"Okay," De Silva started the conversation. "So, here is what we have. We have him on a few counts: Destroying or Concealing of Evidence; Conspiracy; Kidnapping; Solicitation of someone to commit a crime; and at the very least manslaughter for Natalie. He'll be locked up for a while once he's indicted. And we have no doubt he will be, his confession is pretty solid. We did offer to help him, since he was so willing to help us get to Vincent. We'll be going for first-degree murder on Vincent. And with all we have right now, it will give us probable cause to bring him in, based on what Francisco told us. Then, so long as the DA is happy with the case, we've built against him, then we will have him."

"So, how soon will you be going to pick him up?" Justin asked while trying to contain himself.

"Just waiting for the go ahead from upstairs. Once we have the arrest warrant, then we can go pay him a visit and bring him here to show him our lovely facilities," Detective Ortega chimed in. "We will also be paying a visit to Mrs. Florentelli. Since she was the one person to have set this in motion, in order to get Carla, I mean, Marnie, she's got blood on her hands too."

Justin slowly walked over to a window. Being on

the third floor gave him a pretty decent view around town. He looks up to see that the gray clouds are starting to slowly drag themselves and block any chance of the slow rising moon, to shine through. As he watches them make their way across the sky, he can hear the loud rumbling of thunder playing catch up behind them. Trees starting to bend, and give way to the wind bullying through leaves, limbs, and various flowerbeds throughout the front of the building. Funny how all this stormy weather could have one assume that once you're in it, it would be cold. Not here though. It's like taking a shower inside of a wet sauna. It could be raining cats and dogs at midnight, with a temperature of 100 degrees, and the humidity will be just as high. Not exactly comfortable when you're forced to take a couple of showers just to get cool again.

He's reminded of the many times back home in San Diego, when he would find his mom sitting out on their patio in the backyard during a rainstorm. How she loved the smell of it. That ever-present smell of wet dirt. Nature's way of bathing all it touches. One of the very last memories he had of her before he was arrested, was when she asked him to sit outside with her. She said his dad didn't have the patience to just sit with her and enjoy nature's own way of allowing a person to tap into senses that we don't take enough time to use in our daily lives. Looking back now, he realizes that she was somewhat of a spiritual nature-minded person, which would explain what he was told about her dabbling in the world of witchcraft. Something he will most certainly explore to find some answers as to why, or how, he has this insane ability of seeing all those names. What really strikes him, is the irony of it all too. That he of all people, could very well be chosen to help lead the way to getting the justice all those victims, so richly deserve. Everything happens for a reason. His mom… his mom… nobody else's mom… HIS mom… always said that to him. That since there is always a reason something good, or bad, happens; he'd make sure that from now on, his reason for the choices he made would be for good. Sometimes though, you can't have good without the bad.

"All right. It's good to have those in higher positions, important positions, owing a favor or two, because we now have our arrest warrant." De Silva spoke out loudly so that he would snap out of wherever his thoughts had him. "Let's go get us our bad guy and get this wrapped up, quickly, safely, and as best we can so we can put him away for good."

"Yes please. I'm starving." Ortega exclaims, which comes as no surprise to anyone else. The other two detectives exchange glances while rolling their eyes, and laughing. Justin smiles as he walks back towards them. Hands in his pockets, trying to hide his anxiety. Keeping his fingers crossed that all goes well, and that Vincent will be easy to round up and haul in, without incident.

"Listen Justin." Hewitt says to him as they all make

their way to the elevator. "We all know how badly you want this guy. We do too. But, no matter how badly you want him, just make sure you don't get overly anxious and do something that could put yourself, or us, in danger. Deal?"

Justin stared back at him for a few moments. Taking just a few seconds to think, before actually saying anything.

"Don't worry. I won't." He spoke before hanging his head down, and looked at the floor. Just then the elevator doors opened, and they all stepped aside to allow people to exit from it.

"When we get to the car, we want you to put on a Kevlar vest okay? Hopefully things won't be bad enough to where it comes in use, but, just in case."

Justin stared blankly at him before saying, "Yeah, I understand. And don't worry. I'll leave the heavy stuff to the three of you."

"Okay. Good. Look, I know you may think that since you were in prison, you'll understand the mind of a criminal. But, no matter how much you may think you know about what a criminal will, or won't do, you have got to remind yourself that you don't. Everyone is different. The minute you get comfortable and relaxed in situations like this, or think you know what to expect, is when mistakes are made. Let's make sure that doesn't happen okay? Vincent is dangerous. We know that. He may already be expecting us to track him down. Especially after our visit to the Massucci house. I'm sure they don't get a lot of visitors out there." De Silva advises him before pressing the "G" button in the elevator.

"Yeah, probably not."

"So, he is most likely, on edge. Just waiting for the other shoe to drop... so to speak."

"What about Mr. Massucci? How do you know he won't give a heads up to Vincent? You know, to give him a head start in getting away?"

"Yeah, no need to worry about that." De Silva said while looking over at Ortega.

"Why do you say that? How can you be so sure?"

"Because in one of my trips to the soda machine during our interview with Francisco, I reached out to a couple of other detective friends of ours, and asked them to take a drive out to Massucci Land and sit on him. Since it's a bit of a drive out there, I told them to leave right away, since it takes forever and a day to get there. They'll let us know when they get there, and if anything happens once they are there," Ortega said while they all exited the elevator and headed out the front entrance.

Justin stared right back at her, appreciating the fact that the responsibility of thinking ahead was not left up to him. Because right now the only thing he was thinking about was seeing Vincent sitting on a pair of handcuffs in the back of a police car. For starters anyway.

Chapter 46

After only driving for about thirty minutes, Detective Ortega got a call on her cell phone from one of the detectives that had been keeping an eye on the Massucci home. Everyone watched her face for any decipherable facial expressions.

She was silent for a few moments, before saying, "Okay, thanks we'll take it from here."

The sound of several proverbial pins dropped, before she said anything to De Silva, who was behind the wheel.

"We need to get to a place on the opposite side of the road, somewhere near a bottleneck stretch from where the Massucci home is."

"What happened?" De Silva said with noticeable concern in her voice.

Justin felt his blood pressure begin to rise, as he now started to get nervous. Hewitt squirmed in his seat as well, sensing the now noticeable tension in the air.

"Vincent left the house in a hurry. DJ said that he drove out in a hurry, and is headed towards town. Well, towards us, I mean."

"So, like you said, we need to get to somewhere between here, and there, someplace that has a bottleneck at the edge of town. From their house." De Silva drove a little faster for a few minutes before she made a quick U-turn.

She saw a clearing on the side of the road. She pulled the car over, and slowly drove it to a spot where she put it in park, so they could wait.

The moon slowly rose behind them, as they waited for Vincent's car to drive by them.

"Your buddy DJ did tell you which car he was driving, right?" Hewitt asked from the backseat.

"Yeah, she did. It's been a while since she called, so we should be seeing his car go by any minute now. This is the only way into town from there, so I don't think we'll be seeing too many cars driving through here right now," Ortega explained to everyone. "DJ said she is behind him, but not close enough to where her, and her partner would be noticed. He's in a late model black Jag."

Just as she was finishing her sentence, they saw Vincent drive by them. Detective Ortega's buddy DJ advised that he drove by them, recognizing their car on the side of the road. DJ said she'd stay behind him and then turn off somewhere once in town, so that De Silva could then take over the tail from there. That would keep him from being suspicious of anyone following him.

Once they got a few minutes into town, Vincent drove down a busy street and pulled over in front of a strip mall. He got out and looked around, as if he were looking for someone. He then walked into a bar that looked small from the outside, but more than likely extended far back from the street.

De Silva drove past his car, and parked on the next block over. They slowly got out of the car, one by one. They all walked to the back of the car, and stood around the rear of it, beside the trunk.

"All right. Look. We go in. Do not approach him. I will do that. Once we're inside, let's spread out. But not so that we can't see each other. Keep eye contact with each other as best you can." De Silva gave out the instructions. "Justin. Though we gave you a Kevlar vest, I can't let you go in with us."

"What do you mean not go in with you? It's a public place!"

She gave a quick look to Ortega, and Hewitt. "Yes, I know it's a public place. But he no doubt is a little spooked. I'd be very surprised if he wasn't. His casual entrance kind of lends to the idea that maybe daddy Damon didn't say anything to him before he left the interview room, or at all."

"I asked DJ and her partner to lend a hand. So, they're going to plant themselves at both the main entrance, and rear as well. He's definitely going to recognize us, so if he sees us before we see him, he may bolt." Ortega advises everyone.

"So, what I am supposed to do? Just sit my ass in the car? Why do I need a vest then, if you don't want me to go in?" Justin showed his disapproval through his facial expressions and words.

"All right, you can go in. I just don't want you to give into your emotions, and get yourself, or someone else, hurt as a result. We need to do this as by the book as we can. We need to bring him in, and get him to talk to us…"

"Okay… okay… I get it… I'll be careful… I won't spook him. We're wasting time as it is." Justin took his frustration, and himself, towards the entrance of the bar. God, he was glad they didn't hand him a gun. He'd for sure use it at this point. Though he wanted to give in to his belief of 'an eye for an eye,' he would try to keep it in check.

Chapter 47

They walked into the entrance, and made their way separately to the four corners of the place, as best they could. There was a good amount of people that were making it somewhat difficult to spot Vincent. Hard to spot him for most people, but not for Justin.

He moved slowly through the crowd. The space itself was larger than it appeared from the outside. Making his way to one of the bars, he went up to an empty bar stool, sitting down with his back to the bar. One of the bartenders got his attention by shouting, "What can I get you?" at him. He ordered a beer, hoping this all would end before his money did.

He scanned the crowd, not seeing anybody that stood out. Nobody here with names or dates shining brightly for him. For only him. Which overall, in the grand scheme of things, was a good thing. He was slowly starting to embrace this crazy ability of his. Now, he just needed it to come through for him. As he was glancing around the many different faces, he saw Detective Hewitt standing near the rear of the bar, close to the restrooms. He was doing all he could to keep him in his peripheral vision, which proved to be challenging through the crowds. The loud music would be distracting as well. Let alone the scantily dressed women. Distractions all around. At least he and the detectives were all dressed well enough to blend in.

"Here you go," the bartender said while sliding the icy cold beer bottle towards him. "That'll be $6.50."

"Damn," Justin said while turning back towards the bartender. "Did you have to fly it in special or something? And if not, where are the other five bottles that should come with it for that price?" The bartender just stared blankly back at him. Justin gave in, reached into his pocket and tossed a $10 bill on the counter. Waiting for his change, he picked up the beer bottle and began to take a sip when something caught his eye in the reflection in the mirror that was hanging on the wall across from him. Moving as if in slow motion, from the restrooms, over to a group of people seated against the wall in a rather secluded corner of the bar. Just what he was looking for. That shining little beacon. And that beacon was on the one and only person that he was focused on finding.

Vincent. The carrier of Justin's only purpose in life right now. Justice. Vincent slithered over and sat down very casually, clearly not appearing to have any concern for anything. Daddy Damon must not have told him anything. Maybe Daddy Damon didn't want to involve himself. To have yet someone else that could tarnish his name. Bad enough his true son had almost given his reputation a black eye. He didn't need someone who was like a son to him doing the same.

Justin held onto his beer bottle, stepped off his bar stool, and started to walk away from the bar when the bartender came back with his change. "Hey buddy, don't forget your change." The bartender placed it on the bar counter in front of him, then stood there staring at the three singles and two quarters, then back up at Justin with a smile. Justin looked down at his change, then back up at the bartender. "Sorry, I'll need all the money I can get, so I can afford a second beer." With that he scooped up all his change, pushed it down into his front pocket, turned away from the bar and started to make his way towards Vincent.

Before he got too close to Vincent, he looked around for the detectives, any of them. So much for keeping eye contact with each other. He lost Hewitt, and didn't know where De Silva, or Ortega went to. Maybe they were making their way through the dance floor or the ever-growing crowd.

He hesitated in contacting any of the detectives via a text message yet. So, he kept both eyes on Vincent for a few minutes, which for him wasn't too difficult, just to make sure Vincent didn't show any signs of leaving. He could be looking at the people around him, or even away from him, and he would still see Vincent. Like following a bouncing ball.

He went and stood near the restrooms that he saw Vincent come out of, which weren't too far away from where he now sat. Just then he saw one of the detectives, and nodded his head in a way that would indicate to come over to where he was.

Very casually, and with every attempt to not be seen or stand out from the crowd, that detective wove their way towards Justin.

"What's going on? Everything okay?" De Silva asked him without hesitation.

"He's sitting over there with about five other people. Two other guys, and three women. He's wearing what appears to be a black silk button-down shirt and tan dress slacks."

De Silva casually looked over at the table that Justin was talking about and saw Vincent, laughing and having a grand time. No doubt Justin was wishing he could silence him permanently, all by himself. She reached into the back pocket of her pants for her cell phone. Typing discreetly, she notified Ortega. She asked her to meet them near the restrooms, on the west side of the dance floor.

With both women now standing next to him, Justin started to feel a little better about their ability to bring Vincent in without incident. Now that they knew where he was, and they were in a somewhat controlled location, he wasn't so concerned about this entire ordeal being dragged out.

Both detectives advised him to stay where he was, and to just watch them from there. Also, to go ahead and text Hewitt to fill him in. That once they started to walk out with Vincent, then he could follow them out. Justin didn't want to ruin their opportunity of getting him out of this place and over to the department for questioning. He wanted to make sure he did what he could, so as not to interfere. No way would he be responsible for causing any delay in getting Vincent behind bars.

He watched the two women detectives slowly make their way over to Vincent's table. While they were on their way over, he sent a text message to Hewitt, telling him to watch for the women at the entrance. Hewitt replied that he would go and wait in front of it, next to the bouncer. Justin looked up from his phone, and looked over at the table where Vincent was now standing with his arms folded across his chest. De Silva and Ortega were facing him, clearly talking to him, but he couldn't hear or tell what, since all he saw were the backs of their heads. Vincent had the most annoying smirk on his face. He started to walk towards them. He could then hear that Vincent was starting to get a little bit of attitude and slightly defensive with both detectives. So, he started to make his way towards the table, close enough to where Vincent would be able to see him.

"I should have known you'd be close by somewhere." Vincent said as he looked over the shoulders of the detectives. "So, no flying solo tonight… huh… car boy? Had to bring reinforcements with you?"

"Don't need reinforcements when I'm looking at someone who loves to ride someone else's coattails. Since you have such a tough time remembering my real name, that's 'Mr.' car boy to you." Justin refused to let this cocky s.o.b. think he could intimidate him. He was clearly just trying to show off in front of the other men, and women.

"Okay. That's enough." De Silva jumped in to make sure this didn't attract more than the attention it was already getting. "Vincent, why don't we step outside and let these folks enjoy the rest of their evening? Detective Ortega and I, have already told you we have a warrant for your arrest, so let's not make this a bigger scene than…"

Before she could finish her sentence, Vincent shoved her into Justin, who caught her before she hit the ground. Detective Ortega got knocked to the ground as Vincent ran right into and over her. He bolted through the crowd towards the main entrance. People started screaming and shouting, but nobody made any attempt to stop him. Both detectives got up after some help from Justin. The three of them took off after Vincent. De Silva used her phone as a walkie talkie and notified Detective DJ to head to the front.

Vincent ran over, ran down, and ran through every and anyone that stood in his way. Even Detective Hewitt couldn't stop him. It was as if he was juiced up on a dozen energy drinks, the way he was barreling through. Hewitt called for back-up, and advised they were all in a foot pursuit now. Giving a description of what Vincent was wearing, they all tore out of the club and off through the foot traffic that was typical of a Florida evening like tonight.

Justin tried his best to keep up with them all. Realizing he wouldn't be able to, he also realized he had an advantage that they don't. He saw the direction that the detectives took off in, so he grabbed a cab, and told the cab driver to drive in that direction. He had the cab drive for a few blocks, asking him to drive around a few corners and alleys.

Knowing the detectives were far behind, he had the cab take one last turn around the corner of the same second block they had already driven through. Keeping his eyes peeled, he finally saw Vincent. He told the cab driver pull over, just past the alleyway that he saw him in. After he paid his cab fare, he got out, and slowly started to walk back to where he saw him.

Crouching down, he inched his way, with his back against the wall of the building next to the alleyway that he was certain Vincent was hiding in. He slowly peeked around the corner, and saw him pacing, while talking on a cell phone. He might have outrun the detectives, but people like him would never outrun someone like Justin. Time to get some justice done.

Chapter 48

Justin reached into his front left pant pocket for his cell phone, and sent a text message to Detective Hewitt as to his location. Hewitt answered back, and demanded that Justin not do anything that would jeopardize them catching Vincent, or get hurt. After Justin gave him his word, he ended his text with two words, "You're welcome." He then put his cell phone back in his front pocket.

He stood back up, and listened to Vincent shouting and complaining to someone on the other end of the conversation.

Looking around, Justin watched traffic go by, both car and foot. He saw a car park a few car lengths away from where he was. Recognizing it, he saw the detectives slowly exit it, and then saw Ortega draw her gun, placing both hands tightly around the grip. Holding it close to her body, she aimed it towards the ground, then quietly and swiftly made her way around the back of the building, so that she could provide cover at the other end of the alley, with Detective DJ right behind her to assist.

Just then, Detectives De Silva and Hewitt ran up as quietly as they could to the corner of the building opposite from where Justin was standing. De Silva placed her index finger against her lips, motioning to Justin to stay quiet, and to get down. Both detectives had their guns in hand, just like Ortega and Detective DJ.

They motioned for him to stay where he was, as he saw two police cruisers drive up. Both drove up slowly, without their lights flashing at all, so that Vincent wouldn't see the reflection of them off the building walls, or anywhere else for that matter.

Justin grabbed his cell phone again, so he could type a message to Detective Hewitt. As he typed his last letter and hit send, he stood up, and slowly started to quietly enter the alleyway where Vincent was still pacing and arguing with what appeared to be the same person. De Silva saw him move towards Vincent, and frantically motioned for him to stop. Hewitt then showed her the text message that Justin sent. "I'm going to go in, because once he sees either of you, he'll probably try and bolt again. Once I have him distracted, then you're welcomed to join the conversation. He can't be stupid enough to be armed. Either way give me about five minutes, then come on in." De Silva gritted her teeth, then advised everyone to go in four minutes.

"Hey. Dumb ass!" Justin shouted out to a very surprised Vincent.

Vincent practically gave himself a case of whiplash by turning around so quickly. "Well, lookie here. What the hell you are doing here car boy? And how did you find me?" Vincent immediately hung up on whoever was on the other line. Stuffing his cell phone in his back pocket, he started walking towards Justin.

"Oh, you weren't that hard to find. I just had to follow the scent of that shitty cologne you have on. Could smell you a mile away."

"Ha!! You're a funny guy, car boy." He started to slowly walk towards Justin. "So, trying on that pair of big boy pants, and thought you'd come after me on your own? Or are your friends nearby?"

"I don't need any help in kicking your ass. I can do that all on my own."

"Ha! Listen to you! What the hell is your beef anyway? I don't even know you." Vincent continued his walk towards him, shortening the distance between them.

"You'll find out soon enough what my 'beef' is. I'll give you a hint. Marnie Ancin."

"Marnie Ancin? Who the hell is that? Don't even know anyone by that name."

"Kind of figured you wouldn't remember. Guys like you don't give a shit about a person's name, if all they're going to do is kill them. I should know, because I used to be one of those guys."

"You? Kill someone? Now that is funny. Listen car boy, if it's because of that chick that we were both going for the other night... I didn't do anything to her... so if she got killed it wasn't by my hands."

"Not that 'chick' I'm talking about a woman you

actually did kill. You and Francisco."

Vincent stopped in his tracks and stood within about fifteen feet in front of Justin, staying silent for a few moments while he replayed what Justin was reminding him of. After he searched his memory bank, he then remembered exactly who Justin was talking about.

"Yeah, I remember now. Shit. That was nothing but business, man."

"Business, huh?"

"That's right, business. Business that didn't have anything to do with you. So, why don't you and your detective friends pack your things, and go back to wherever you came from?"

"Well see, that's just it. Your business does have something to do with me. That was my mom you killed. So yeah. I'm not going anywhere until I see you get exactly what you deserve."

Vincent didn't say anything for a few moments, trying to gather his thoughts, his words, while staring straight into Justin's eyes. Justin did not even so much as blink, matching death stare for death stare.

"Well shit," Vincent said, and stood still with his arms crossed across his chest, trying to show that he could care less about Justin, or how Justin felt. "That was your mom? Ha! Small world. That explains what you're doing here then. I will say this, women like your mom should know better than to run out on their man like that. At least that's what I was told she did. You saying you've done the same thing, then you should know what I'm talking about. Besides, she made me a lot of money, I will say that. Don't know about Francisco. He's the one that got me the gig. You should probably talk to him about that too, you know. She went really easy, you know? She knew she was in trouble the minute he and I walked up to her. I will say this, she put up a little bit of a fight. Not enough to save herself though. Of course." They both glared at each other without either one of them moving. Justin tapped into every ounce of restraint that he could. "Too bad too. Your mom was quite the looker. I bet she was a heartbreaker when she was younger. Soft skin too. In the meantime, what're you going to do about it… car boy?" With that he took a couple steps closer to him.

Before Justin had the chance to rip Vincent's throat out with his bare hands, the detectives and officers came charging in with their guns drawn, yelling at Vincent to drop to his knees. Giving him instructions to sprawl out on his belly, with his arms stretched on either side, palms up, feet crossed over each other, Detective Ortega ran over to him, placed one knee on his back, pulled both hands behind his back, then slapped a pair of cuffs on his wrists. "Vincent Marino, you're under arrest for the murder of Marnie Isabel Ancin. Get up!" She grabbed one of his arms with both hands while she mirandized him.

After she helped him stand up, he boasted out loud, "Why waste your time, people? You know I'll be out in an hour. You forget who I work for."

"Oh, we remember who you work for. Funny thing is, your employer, Mr. Massucci, doesn't want someone working for him that would tarnish his good reputation. So, I'm fairly confident that you won't be out in an hour, but you will be out of a job. Not to mention, on your own with this one," De Silva boasted right back at him. "Get him out of here," she said to Ortega, who then hauled him past Justin to a waiting police unit parked on the street.

"You know, if you guys hadn't charged in when you did, I probably would have started to beat the shit out of him," Justin said to De Silva.

"Yeah, then what? Become a resident of the state again?" she said, while Hewitt walked over and stood next to them both, making sure that the discussion didn't become heated simply because Justin was already worked up. Both detectives then holstered their weapons while the other detectives, and officers around them, did the same before making their way back to their cars.

"It would have been worth it for sure," he replied. "I just wanted to get my own form of justice for my mom. And peace of mind for my dad and I."

"Yes, well, we all appreciate the fact that you chose to listen to common sense, and ignored that impulse," De Silva said to him, before he headed to the end of the alleyway.

As she headed out, she turned to Hewitt and asked

while walking backwards, "By the way, did you or Ortega give him the, uh, 'special vest' to wear?"

"Special vest? There's a special type of vest? What're you talking about? What special vest?" Justin then turned to Hewitt, and asked him, "What is she talking about?"

He looked back at De Silva and replied, "Yes. Yes, I did."

"Good, don't forget to grab what we need before we get to the station."

"Will someone tell me what's going on? What are you guys talking about?" Justin couldn't help but feel like he helped hand them Vincent, but also can't help feeling left out at the same time. ¶

Chapter 49

"We rolled the dice on the off chance that you would take advantage of any opportunity to dig out whatever info you could from Vincent if you had him to yourself... and... well... that happened... and... you did," De Silva began to explain to him. "I mean, we didn't expect it to really happen, but I am glad it did."

"Can you just let me know what you're talking about, please? And what does it have to do with a special vest?"

The detective let out a deep sigh, then asked Justin to take his shirt off so she could help get the Kevlar vest off him. Justin shook his head in confusion, unbuttoned his shirt, then handed it to her. He then started to take off the vest by separating the Velcro straps, while she walked up behind him. She checked the back of the vest and made sure that the part that makes it special was still intact.

"Here, I'll take that." She motioned with her hands out. Justin took off the vest completely, then handed it over to her, in exchange for his shirt. She then reached into a small pocket hidden away near the upper shoulder area, and she pulled out what appeared to be a small transmitter. It was connected to a small wire running through the vest that then led to something that looked like a small microphone.

"I was wearing a wire? Are you serious?" Justin said with shock.

"Yes. You were. We didn't tell you because we didn't want you to act any more nervous than you probably already were. We couldn't tip him off at all. In the off chance that this did take place, we wanted you to act as natural as possible. Without any hesitation or anxiety. Given everything he said to you tonight, it makes a pretty solid case against him now. So, I'd say it was a successful gamble. I'm sorry to have put you in that position, but we had to take that risk."

"Pretty risky gamble!" he said while putting his shirt back on.

"One that definitely paid off. We also kind of figured that Vincent would brag. We knew he'd want to talk about what he did. He has that kind of narcissistic mentality." She wrapped the wire lead around the small transmitter, then held onto the Kevlar vest as she started to walk out of the alleyway, and towards the cars. "C'mon. Let's get going."

Justin followed behind her, right back to the car they all came in.

"For the record, I wasn't nervous. I was angry," he said, as he seated himself in the backseat of the car. "So, you guys knew about the wire as well?" He looked at Detectives Ortega and Hewitt, who were already in the car.

They both looked away with a smirk.

"Sorry, Justin. We were sworn to secrecy," Ortega replied with half a smile on her face. "Kind of our own version of a hail Mary, I guess you'd say."

Justin half frowned, and just stared out of the window. "So now what?"

"Now, we make our case. We've got him on a recording, basically admitting to the fact that he killed her. Now, we listen to what he has to say to us face to face, as to how he was chosen to murder her. I mean, we have Francisco's story, but we want to hear it from him, and see if he'll come clean about it. See if the two stories match," De Silva explained while starting up the car, and then driving away from the curb, in order to get behind the car that now carried Vincent in the backseat.

"I'm guessing the confession of sorts that he gave me will pretty much seal his fate. Won't it?" Justin asked of all the detectives.

"Pretty much. Don't get me wrong, a confession is always going to be something like the holy grail that we as detectives want at the end of the day," Ortega said to him, while turning around to face him from the front seat.

"We know how badly you wanted him, and to get justice. Now that we have him, we also want to get Marco's mom, Mrs. Florentelli. Vincent may have been the one to follow through in taking your mom's life, but Mrs. Florentelli was the one that set this plan in motion, based on what Francisco told us. They all had a choice.

They all chose wrong, and they're now going to have to pay for their actions. But those actions all started with her. So, if we can get him to accept a deal while giving her to us, then this entire case will no longer be open, and we can let your mom rest in the peace she deserves."

"Yeah. Well, that is the very least of what she deserves. Because she sure as hell didn't deserve what happened to her. Not just in what he did to her, but also from what I now know how her first husband Marco treated her. So, it's a good thing he isn't around," he said before looking out the window in silence.

The ride back to the station remained a quiet one. Justin got lost in his thoughts, trying to sort through his emotions. He felt partially vindicated. Partially only because of the fact that Vincent wasn't behind bars… yet. Maybe once that happened, he would feel some level of vindication. Just not fully. Because in order for him to feel that, his mom would have to be back at home when he returned to San Diego. As if Vincent were holding her captive somewhere. There was never going to be complete closure, either. That ache, that break, that crack in his heart might mend, but would never go away. He would have to be satisfied with acceptance. Accepting the fact that she was gone, and would never come home. She would, however, be alive in every single happy moment of every memory he had left of her.

He had to learn to stay positive, if only for his dad. Their lives would truly change, once he was back home for good. He had to remind himself that he did help get the bad guy. He also had to remember to give himself a pat on the back, for helping make that happen. So many things he had to learn to embrace: his past, and his new, present life. He couldn't even think about the future. Living in the here and now would be his new focus.

Looking at the car in front of them, he saw the back of Vincent's head in the backseat. To think that was once him. Pretty insane, this strange turn of events. All the shitty things that had to happen in order for this very moment to take place.

He got the sense that Vincent was probably feeling pretty invincible right about now. Invincible and bulletproof. No doubt the detectives were going to do whatever was within their power to make sure that Vincent didn't get to have a repeat performance by damaging someone else's family. They'd do what they could to make sure he stayed locked up for good. And if not for good, at least for 25 years. ¶

Chapter 50

They all walked into the department and headed to De Silva's office. Justin felt exhausted just from thinking about everything that was about to happen.

"So, where is he?" Justin asked as he and the other detectives take a seat. All except for De Silva.

"He's being brought in and booked, so we can go talk to him and get to know each other really well," Ortega explained. "De Silva is going over to booking, and she'll let me know when he's available to get ourselves acquainted."

"What do I get to do now that you guys have him?"

"Well, to be honest with you, there really isn't much else that you'll have to do here," Ortega said to a very anxious-looking Justin.

"I knew you would say that," he said while standing up, and then began to walk around the room. "You know I want to see this whole thing through. I mean, like the trial and everything."

"You'll be involved, for at least part of it, Justin," Hewitt reassured him. "We both will be. This entire investigation wouldn't even have happened if it weren't for you."

"Yeah, I know, but just because I helped find him,

and you have him in custody, I can't just let that be it. I mean, for now anyway. I don't want to go back home yet, without knowing he is really going to prison for what he did to my mom."

"He's not going anywhere. Don't worry," Ortega said while standing up herself, feeling a little of Justin's anxiety spill over to her. Just then, her phone let out a chime indicating she had a new text message. As she looked down at the screen, she saw it was from De Silva. "Speaking of which. That's De Silva. It's going to be a while. So, why don't you guys go get something to eat? Kinda late now, but there's plenty of places where you can still get some dinner. I would suggest getting something from our super-nutritional vending machines here, although I wouldn't even feed some of that stuff to a transient. Hell, even as hungry as I may get, I won't even eat most of that stuff. I mean, unless I am absolutely famished. Then it's just out of sheer desperation that I'll eat from it," she said with a giggle.

"Yeah, I guess so. I'm going to take a walk. Try to shake off some of this anxiety. I'll check out those few places to eat at." he said to both detectives.

"Why don't we both go, Justin? I'll drive. I'm pretty hungry myself. Ortega, wanna join us?" Hewitt asked.

"You two go ahead. I'll stick around here and start the inevitable pile of paperwork that we'll need to get going. I'll text you when I hear something."

Both men nodded their heads in agreement as they

headed out of the office.

"She'll let us know if there's any problems. But I don't think we have anything to worry about, okay? He's going to have to be extradited back to San Diego, since that is where it happened. We have a rock-solid case against him in my opinon, so I can't imagine he'd fight that." Hewitt said as they both headed out of the building.

"I know. It's just the paranoia that is starting to take hold of me. To get this close, and to have him in the same place, the same building. You know? I mean. I'm one to talk I know, but when it hits this close to home. Karma really is a super bitch."

Detective Hewitt let out a low chuckle. "I know. I'm sure the irony hasn't escaped you at all. There's a little café just down the road a bit. They're open. They picked a pretty good spot to open a business. Especially since they're open twenty-four hours a day. Lots of cops needing a better-tasting coffee. Not to mention a good-tasting meal to go with it."

They drove a couple blocks down the street from police headquarters, and the neighboring jail. Hewitt parked next to the building, and they made their way in. They sat themselves down, just as the sign inside the entrance suggested they do. Making their way over to a small booth, they looked over the menu after turning over the coffee cups sitting in front of them, an indication that they without a doubt wanted some coffee. There was a pretty good amount of people with apparently the same idea and appetite inside the café with them.

A middle-aged waitress walked over to their table, carrying a fresh pot of coffee, and began to pour some into their cups.

"Hi gents. What can I get you? Or do you need some time look over the menu?"

"No, I'll have a BLT, French fries, and a diet soda," Hewitt said to her.

"I'll have the same," Justin said before she thanked them both, then took both menus and walked away to turn in their orders.

Both men looked around the place, as if they were scoping it out for something, or someone. Especially Justin.

"Pretty busy place tonight," Justin said as he looked around the place. He saw a lot of police officers mixed in with a lot of civilians. Unless those civilians were undercover.

"Yeah, it was always busy whenever the detectives and I would come here, too. When I was out here before. Told you, they picked the perfect location for this place."

As they sat there with their coffee, Justin couldn't help but notice a couple sitting near the end of the counter. Young couple, maybe in their early 30s, seeing them in the only way he can. They were clearly nervous, too. He was the only one that noticed, though.

"Hewitt."

"Yeah?"

"Got something to write with?"

"Um, yeah... hang on..." Hewitt patted his left shirt pocket, with the palm of his right hand.

"Not for me... for you."

"What?"

"Write these names down."

Hewitt stays staring at Justin, speechless. Slowly realizing the only reason, he would tell him to write names down. It was something he still hadn't quite gotten used to. Something he might never get used to. Clearly Justin was getting used to his gift.

"Sammi R. Taylor. 5132008." He paused for a moment before he said the next name. "Lexi A. Taylor. 5132008. Both names are on the guy."

"Got it." Hewitt jotted the names and date down in a notepad he had inside an inner pocket of his coat. "Shit. Same last name. Same date. Twins maybe. Where is he sitting?"

"At the end of the counter, young-looking couple. Man, and a woman."

"Okay, listen." He closed the notepad, and replaced it back inside his coat pocket, as well as his pen. "You stay here, I'm going to go over to the counter, so I can get a little closer to them, and see if I can just have someone give me a coffee pot that we can keep at our table. That way I can get a good look at them. We're going to need a good description when we get back."

"Yeah... okay." Justin stayed in his seat, and

casually drank from his cup of coffee. Even if Hewitt was pretending to get the coffee pot, he should get it anyway. Gonna be another long night again. He could definitely see that now.

They didn't leave right away from the café after they finished their meals, so that they could keep an eye on the young couple and maybe catch where they went afterwards. Once they saw them leave, they watched them through the windows as best they could. Hewitt got the info of the car they got into, which was parked under a lamp in the parking lot, giving him a better look at it. They were either not very bright for picking a café so close to the police station, or they weren't locals. Either way, their running would soon be over.

Chapter 51

They got back to the station without having heard anything from either De Silva, or Ortega, throughout the entire time they were gone.

Heading straight for De Silva's office, they found Ortega sitting behind the desk, busily tapping away at the keyboard.

"There you guys are. I was just about to text you. De Silva literally just told me that Vincent gave up everything. After we confirmed for him that his wonderful employer, Mr. Massucci, wouldn't be paying his way out, he was all too willing to help us. Guess he didn't like the fact that his new accommodations didn't have his favorite silk sheets. So, he said whatever he needed to, in order to make his stay at the state-provided suites, as short as possible." Neither man responded right away. "What? I thought you'd be glad to hear that? Look, I'm sorry I didn't text you. That's because they brought him out like thirty minutes after you left. And De Silva didn't want to waste any time. Thought you'd want to take your time eating anyway, it's been a long day. Besides…"

"I saw some people at the café we went to," Justin said, interrupting her.

"Yeah, that is what one usually sees in a café," she answered back with a grin.

"No, what he means is he *saw* people," Hewitt clarified.

Ortega looked back and forth between the two men, before ending her shocked look on Justin. "Oh! Shit! Sorry! Who'd you see? I mean, whose name? Did you get a good look at the guy? I mean, assuming it was a guy."

"It was a guy and a girl. Two names. Same last name, on the same date," Justin told her.

"Oh, damn! Really? Two people? I mean, two names? On the two people? Were these two people with each other?"

"Yeah, they were. They were already there when we got there. I didn't see them until we sat down."

"I got a good look at them, so I'll be able to identify them, after we check out the names first," Hewitt explained to her. He walked over to join her behind the desk, while Justin slowly sat himself down on one of the chairs. He was suddenly very exhausted.

"You okay, Justin? You look a little out of it," she asked after noticing the seriousness of his face. She got up and walked towards him, while Hewitt took over on the keyboard.

"Yeah, I'm fine. Just a little overwhelmed right now. Dealing with Vincent, and now this. It's just all a little crazy. It's just all starting to sink in, I guess. I'm just a little tired, is all." He put his face in his hands, and kept his eyes shut.

"Hey..." Ortega pulled up a chair next to him. Placing her hand on his back, she asked him if he wants some water.

"No, I'm okay." He brought his head back up, and took in a deep breath, while rubbing his hands back and forth on both knees. "I just need to sit here for a few minutes."

"Yeah, sure. Just take it easy for a bit. I'm going to get you some water anyway. Don't want you to get dehydrated at all. Anxiety can do that, along with all the stress. Sit tight. I'll be right back." She exchanged glances with Hewitt, then walked out to get some water.

Other than the usual noise that a police department might have, it had now turned into a torrential downpour outside. Even at the late hour that it was, there were still of course the officers and detectives that were dedicated to finding the bad guys in any case they might be working on. Detectives Hewitt, Ortega, and De Silva were no exception.

As Justin was sitting there, not only trying to calm his nerves, but trying to get his entire body to just relax, he was going over in his mind everything that had just happened. He watched Hewitt work on getting info on the two people they had encountered at the café. He regretted not being there at the time that Vincent was brought in and questioned. The absolute pleasure he would have taken in seeing him in handcuffs and with no chance of getting away again.

Chapter 52

Detective Ortega returned with a pitcher of water and some Styrofoam cups. Justin got up and stretched, trying to get his blood flowing at the right speed and to all the right places. He was starting to feel lightheaded, most likely due to just allowing himself to get overwhelmed with everything.

"Thanks for the water," he said to Ortega, while pouring himself a cup of it.

"Yeah, of course." She looked at him, concerned that all of this was too much for him.

"Where is De Silva?" he asked while drinking down an entire cup of water.

"She's putting the finishing touches on Vincent's case. She should be in here in a few minutes."

As she finished saying that, De Silva walked in, feeling very accomplished and very happy to be walking in her office after nabbing the person responsible for Marnie's murder.

"Hey… what's going on?" she said as she saw Hewitt busily researching on her computer. "Looking very serious over there, Hewitt. Something wrong?"

"No, he's good. He and Justin encountered some folks that he's checking on right now. But we can get to that in a few. What's going on with Vincent?"

"Is it a done deal? He's toast, right?" Justin said excitedly now.

"Pretty much, yeah. We offered him a plea deal. Kidnapping, and first-degree murder. He told us how Mrs. Florentelli was so angry, with how Carla broke Marco's heart, which she feels led to his suicide, that she wanted revenge. We'll go with Kidnapping as opposed to Aggravated Kidnapping. He'll definitely do time, a lot of it. We're also going to throw in assault and battery for good measure. If we drop the assault and battery, maybe he'll feel like he's getting a better deal and not put up as much as a fight."

"Was he putting up much of a fight anyway?" Justin asked.

"Honestly, no. He was surprisingly super humble." She responded before walking over to the pitcher of water that was sitting on the corner of her desk, and poured a cup for herself, then sat down across from the desk. She didn't want to interrupt the intense work that Hewitt seemed to be so deeply involved in. "I think part of it is out of respect for Mr. Massucci. Well, in a strange round about, sort of way anyway."

"You mean, respecting his reputation, in a sort of twisted way, showing his appreciation for all he's done for him? So, for that reason he didn't want to drag him into his mess," Ortega suggested.

"Exactly."

"Well, whatever it is, I'm glad he's been arrested at

all," Justin said before getting some more water.

"Hey, you okay? You don't look so hot," De Silva asked Justin as he returned to the chair he was sitting in.

"Yeah, I was feeling a little dehydrated a while ago. But uh... I'm good now."

"So, we'll get it all wrapped up here with a nice big bow, and get the DA to review everything, and take it from there. Get him extradited to California. Go to trial. It'll no doubt be a while before that happens. The trial that is"

"So, what... I just head back to San Diego? I can't do anything else here?"

"Well... uh... we have Vincent in custody now. He's given us what we need to keep him locked up. We won't need you until we go to trial. I know that doesn't sound right to you, as far as you being needed and all. I mean, you've given us unmeasurable help. You gotta know that," De Silva said with as much sensitivity as she could muster up.

"Yeah, I know. I wouldn't have been able to get this far without you guys, either. I am probably the last person you'd be expecting to show gratitude for you, but I am truly grateful for you guys. I honestly am. So, thanks for all your help."

"Well, you can thank us once he's sentenced. That'll definitely be the final nail in his coffin," Ortega commented.

"Got it!" Hewitt shouted from behind De Silva's desk. "I found out who belonged to the two names."

"So, what'd you find?" Ortega was practically salivating while joining Hewitt behind the desk. Looking over his shoulder at what he found in his search, she said, "Oh. Shit. That is not what I expected you to find. At least, not from your description of the two people that you both saw."

"Okay, now that you all know what's going on with Vincent, you want to fill me in on the what and the who?" De Silva now said with a small amount of anxiety.

"The two people that Justin noticed had two different names that lit up for him. Both on the male. Different first names, but the same last name." Hewitt started to explain while still reading info on the computer screen.

"All right. And... what?" De Silva said, wishing she could pull the words out of Hewitt.

"The two we saw reported their twin daughters missing back in May of 2008. Parents are a Don and Laura Taylor of Santee, South Carolina. Reported their four-year-old daughters missing in the early hours of May 13, 2008. Both parents questioned of course, for hours on end after their call in to police."

"I'm guessing they didn't have enough to pursue the mom and dad with at the time, I gather?" asked De Silva, while looking over at Justin to gauge his reaction after hearing that information.

"Parents were never charged. They claimed that they put the girls to bed the night before, woke up the next morning, and that's when they discovered that the girls were gone. They called 911. Police did a sweep of the place top to bottom. Only sign of any forced entry was a busted window, and a busted-up torn screen. And yeah, nothing concrete, from any of the forensic evidence, of which there wasn't very much. Authorities suspected the parents, but didn't have enough to tie them to the kids' disappearance. Bodies were never found. They fear that their bodies may have been dumped in nearby Lake Marion, and if so, that would be why they never found them. Parents didn't have any record, just some domestic issues."

"Okay, so, contact the arresting officers, find out who ended up with the case. We'll let them know that the parents were spotted here. We don't want to go too far into why or how we discovered their case in our backyard. We'll take it from there after talking to them," De Silva instructed.

"You got it. I'll print out what we have here, and give them a call tomorrow." Hewitt then did a few clicks on what he had in front of him, and walked over to the nearby printer to collect the pages.

"Actually, Hewitt?"

"Yeah?"

"Why don't you leave that with us? Ortega and I will follow up on it for you, and let you know if and when we need your help. You're going to have your hands full with Vincent once he's extradited over there to stand trial, and we'll be happy to hand him off to you.

We have enough bad guys like him here in Florida. We don't need any more," she said with half a grin. Ortega shared in smiling back at both gentlemen as well, showing her approval of De Silva's offer.

Hewitt smiled back in agreement. He handed her the copies of the Taylor case, then looked over at Justin. He walked over to him and patted him on his shoulder.

"You feeling all right? Ready to head back over to the hotel now?" he asked.

"Yeah, I'm all right. I guess I am pretty exhausted. I may actually get a full night's sleep tonight. Been kinda wound up," Justin said as he rubbed the back of his neck.

"Well, gee… I can't imagine why," Ortega joked back at him, then smiled.

"We'll call you in the morning before we take off," Hewitt mentioned to both women. "Have a good night, and thanks for everything." He then walked over to them both and gave them each a hug before heading towards the door of the office.

Justin duplicated his actions and walked over to both women and gave them each a kiss on the cheek and a hug. "Thank you so very much for putting your trust in me, and helping me track my mom's killer down."

"You did all the hard work," De Silva said with a wink. "It was our pleasure. Thanks for your help, too."

With that both men headed out of the office, and waved goodbye.

Chapter 53

Since arriving back in San Diego a few weeks after the Florida trip, Justin kept in touch with Detective Hewitt as to the progress of getting Vincent back in town and the pending trial. He kept a very low profile, and took advantage of all the time he had available in getting to know his dad all over again. Getting to know him as a grown man now, and not some confused, floundering teenager.

He had told his dad David about everything that happened in the days before leaving prison. About his new-found talent, and what he discovered about his mom, Marnie. Once the initial shock wore off, they talked about everything related to her. About her life before Marnie. All that had happened in her first marriage. And how everything that happened to her as Carla was what ultimately caught up with her and caused her death as Marnie.

"If I only knew," David had said, after hearing about it all, one morning over breakfast.

"You probably wouldn't have been able to do anything dad. I mean, if you had, you might not be sitting here right now. Hell, I probably wouldn't be either." Justin reassures him. "People like the

Florentellis, and the Massuccis, they don't let people get in their way. Mom didn't matter to them. She wasn't good enough for this Marco guy. At least, that's what Marco's mom thought. So, when he killed himself, his mom set this master plan in motion. Mom was incredibly brave and bold and smart, too. I mean, look at everything she did on her own."

"Yeah, but I can't help but feel some guilt. Just human nature, you know? You take vows to always be there. Through thick and thin. I just wished she had told me, is all," his father said, then just sat quietly, hanging his head down. Twirling his coffee cup, thinking back, in order to see if there were any signs that he might have missed, knowing he would probably go mad trying to think of any.

They spent a few moments in silence. Going through the what ifs in their minds.

"Now this 'thing' that you've discovered about yourself. You say you didn't notice it until you were about to be released?"

"Yeah, I actually noticed it about a year before my release."

"Wow, a whole year before? You never said anything."

"That's because I didn't want anyone to think I was crazy, and give them a reason to keep me longer."

"Ah. Yeah, I totally understand, and get that," his dad said while standing up to refill his coffee. He lifted the coffee pot up in Justin's direction, motioning if he wanted more.

"No, I'm good, thanks." Justin was still drinking from the cup he had. "I noticed it on July 23rd of last year, Dad. Which, as it turns out, was the one-year anniversary of Mom's death. I just didn't know it at the time. I mean, I knew when she died. What didn't occur to me was the date that I started seeing the names. Not until I put some more thought into it. So, that's why I think mom has a hand in all this. Something with that witchcraft stuff, somehow. At least, that's the only explanation I can find for it."

David sat himself back down at the table. He scratched the top of his head in thought. "The most farfetched thing I am positive I've ever heard of. If you weren't my son, I'd find it hard to believe. But I do. Believe you, I mean. I mean, you're my son. Why wouldn't I believe you?"

They stared and smiled at each other, without having to speak any words for a few moments.

"Damn. It's good to have you home, son. Truly."

"Thanks, Dad. It's beyond good to be home. I mean, it's all starting to finally sink in. But... yeah... I'm home."

They both finished their coffee and breakfast, then took their dishes over to the sink, and washed them all out.

"Hey... uh... listen, I am headed into town if you want to come along for the ride. I know you probably haven't had much time to really get used to everything around here. So, if you want to tag along, you're welcome to."

"Thanks, yeah I, uh, told Detective Hewitt I'd meet up with him at the police station to go over some things before Vincent's trial next month. Sorry. Maybe tomorrow?"

"Oh yeah sure." David waved his hand at him, as if to say "don't worry about it." "Tomorrow is fine, or whenever. We have plenty of time to catch you up on places, and things, around here."

"Thanks, Dad. Appreciate it. Catch up with you later then?"

"Of course. Don't sweat it. Talk to you later, son." He smiled and headed out the front door.

Watching his dad leave still seemed so surreal to him. Justin had thought he would never be given a second chance at life again. But he was very grateful for it. It was definitely not lost on him.

Chapter 54

He arrived at the police station about an hour later. He had called Detective Hewitt from home, letting him know approximately when to expect him. Hewitt then met him in the lobby, where their new-found friendship all began.

"So, how's your dad doing? I bet he's happy you're back."

They walked down the hallway, into Hewitt's office.

"Want some coffee or something?" Hewitt then offered him, as soon as they walked in and sat down. Hewitt was drinking from a cup of coffee himself.

"No thanks, I'm good. Any more coffee, and we'll be discussing things from the men's room." Justin laughed while giving his answer.

Both men laughed together at the thought of that.

"Duly noted. No more coffee for Justin today." He snickered back.

They spent the next hour catching up, in between Hewitt briefing him on the details of the upcoming trial, what Justin should expect out of everything, and what he should start to understand as to his role in it.

"We're not anticipating you actually having to

testify, but if you do, it would only be to speak about your mom's character. You know, as to the type of person she was, her life before, basically what you knew her to be like."

"Has the prosecution said anything specific to you?"

"No. Not yet. Which is why I'm not sure how they'll actually play it out, you know?"

"Yeah. Yeah, I hear ya."

After Hewitt went over the rest of what might be happening at the trial, they decided to catch up again about two weeks before the trial.

"You got any plans right now, want to go grab a bite? I drank the rest of my breakfast, as you saw already," Hewitt explained as he started to walk Justin out of the building.

"Yeah, that sounds okay. My dad is running around town here somewhere, so I'll catch up with him at dinner. Lunch sounds good. I mean, lunch for me, breakfast for you."

"Ha. Yeah. Exactly."

Both men slowly made their way down the hall, entering the lobby.

"You know, Justin, I could sure use your help in solving some cold cases. I don't know what kind of jobs you may be looking for, but there's a lot of families out there that would love to have the same kind of closure you're getting. Besides, we already know we work well together. This may be your calling, you never know."

Justin stopped and stared at the detective, contemplating what he just said to him.

"Listen, no pressure. I just thought, you know, I wasn't sure if you had any jobs lined up or anything. At least think about, will you?"

"Yeah. I will. I'll think about it. Give me a few days. I'd like to talk to my dad about it first. You know, get his take on it."

"Of course, yeah. No hurry. You let me know."

As they got closer to the doors, a frantic woman walked in. She stomped her way to the front counter, and slapped her hands down, demanding attention.

"I want some goddamned help! I am so tired of the run around! I want some help!!"

Hewitt asked Justin to wait a minute, so he could see what was going on.

"That's okay, Karen, I got this," Hewitt said to the front desk clerk, while holding his hand up to have her stop. "Ma'am… ma'am…" He tried to calm her down. "My name is Detective Hewitt. What's going on? How can I help?"

Justin slowly started to walk towards Hewitt.

"It's my father. I want help with my father!!" The woman was clearly not calming down as quickly as Hewitt or others around the lobby would like.

"Your father? Okay… what about him?"

"He's dead! He's been dead for over five years, and you people still haven't found his killer! I'm tired of calling all the time, and leaving messages that never get returned! I want answers!"

Hewitt then walked her over to a chair nearby, as a desk clerk walked over a cup of water. The woman drank the water and started to calm down.

"All right. You okay now?"

She took a deep breath before speaking calmly. "Yeah… yeah… I'm okay…"

"Okay. Why don't we start with your name… what's your first name?"

"Catherine?" Justin said with complete and utter shock.

The woman looked up with the same level of disbelief at him.

"Justin? Is that you? Oh my god. I… I… didn't see you there…"

She jumped up and gave him a hug.

"I can't believe it…" She let go and stood there staring at him, head to toe.

Detective Hewitt stood by and watched the drama unfold.

"Do you work here? I thought you were in prison. Wow. From con to ex-con to cop? Ha. Small world for sure. Well maybe you can help me then, if you work here. Please."

Justin was still stunned at what was happening right before his very eyes.

She hadn't changed since high school. Still beautiful. And here she was in front of him. He was immediately taken back to that night they were together.

That one girl. The one he never called back. The one and only girl that he would have loved to see under better circumstances. Small world indeed.

"Detective Hewitt."

Hewitt then walked over to him. "Yes."

"I've thought about it. And it appears we have a case to work on."

Catherine grabbed his hands and kissed them. Yes, it really was a small world, and it was calling his name.

Stay tuned to find out what happens next, now that Justin, and Catherine, have crossed paths again. Will he will be able to help her in her search for justice? Or is his ability only temporary.

CPSIA information can be obtained
at www.ICGtesting.com
Printed in the USA
LVHW030846130521
687330LV00001B/84